P9-EGM-253

BEST LOVED BOOKS
FOR YOUNG READERS

The Adventures of Tom Sawyer

A CONDENSATION OF THE BOOK BY

Mark Twain

Illustrated by John Falter

CHOICE PUBLISHING, INC.
New York

The condensation in this volume has been created by The Reader's Digest Association, Inc.

PRODUCED IN ASSOCIATION WITH MEDIA PROJECTS INCORPORATED

Executive Editor, Carter Smith
Managing Editor, Jeanette Mall
Project Editor, Jacqueline Ogburn
Associate Editor, Charles Wills
Contributing Editor, Elizabeth Prince
Art Director, Bernard Schleifer

Library of Congress Catalog Number: 88-63347
ISBN: 0-945260-19-9

This 1989 edition is published and distributed by Choice Publishing, Inc., Great Neck, NY 11021, with permission of The Reader's Digest Association, Inc.

Manufactured in the United States of America.

10 9 8 7 6 5 4 3 2

OTHER TITLES IN THE

Reader's Digest

BEST LOVED BOOKS
FOR YOUNG READERS

SERIES

The Merry Adventures of Robin Hood by Howard Pyle
Alice's Adventures in Wonderland and
Through the Looking Glass by Lewis Carroll
Great Cases of Sherlock Holmes by Sir Arthur Conan Doyle
Treasure Island by Robert Louis Stevenson
Tales of Poe by Edgar Allan Poe
Little Women by Louisa May Alcott
The Jungle Books by Rudyard Kipling
The Life and Strange Surprising Adventures of Robinson Crusoe by Daniel Defoe
The Call of the Wild by Jack London and
Typhoon by Joseph Conrad
Twenty Thousand Leagues Under the Sea by Jules Verne
The Adventures of Huckleberry Finn by Mark Twain
The Story of King Arthur and His Knights by Howard Pyle
Kidnapped by Robert Louis Stevenson
Beau Geste by Percival Christopher Wren
The Red Badge of Courage by Stephen Crane

Foreword

For Tom Sawyer, adventure was always just around the corner. Sometimes, tired of being the respectable boy his kindly but harassed Aunt Polly felt he should be, he sneaked out in the dark of night to seek excitement with his wonderful unrespectable friend, Huck Finn. Sometimes adventure came to him by accident—when he witnessed a murder in a lonely cemetery, was surprised by "ghosts" in a haunted house, and got lost in a labyrinthine cave with the bewitching Becky Thatcher. His was a joyous life, filled with feuds and friendships, with crazy jokes, narrow escapes, and splendid schemes.

Mark Twain, author of this classic story of American boyhood, said in a preface to the 1876 edition: "Most of the adventures recorded in this book really occurred: one or two were experiences of my own, the rest those of boys who were schoolmates of mine. Huck Finn is drawn from life; Tom Sawyer also, but not from an individual—he is a combination of the characteristics of three boys who I knew. The odd superstitions touched upon were all prevalent among children and slaves in the West at the period of this story."

Born in Florida, Missouri, in 1835, Mark Twain grew up in Hannibal, a sleepy little town on the banks of the Mississippi River very like Tom's St. Petersburg. His real name was Samuel Langhorne Clemens; and he took his pen name from the call of the riverboat hands that meant two fathoms on the sounding line. In his long and varied career he was a printer, a steamboat pilot, a silver miner, a journalist, and finally a successful writer and lecturer.

Mark Twain traveled far from Hannibal, and the mane of white hair that characterized him in his later years was as well known in Vienna and London as in the cities of the United States. He died, at the age of seventy-five, in his home in Redding, Connecticut. But when we think of him today, we think of the Middle West in the days before the Civil War, of *The Adventures of Tom Sawyer*, of its equally famous sequel, *The Adventures of Huckleberry Finn*, and *Life on the Mississippi*, in all of which a way of life now past is vividly immortalized.

CHAPTER I

"Tom!"

No answer.

"Tom!"

No answer.

"What's gone with that boy, I wonder? You TOM!"

No answer.

The old lady pulled her spectacles down and looked over them about the room; then she put them up and looked out under them. She seldom or never looked *through* them for so small a thing as a boy; they were her state pair, the pride of her heart, and were built for "style," not service—she could have seen through a pair of stove lids just as well. She looked perplexed, and then said, not fiercely but still loud enough for the furniture to hear:

"Well, I lay if I get hold of you I'll—"

She did not finish, for by this time she was punching under the bed with the broom, and needed breath to punctuate the punches with. She resurrected nothing but the cat.

"I never did see the beat of that boy!" She went to the open door and lifted up her voice: "Y-o-u-u *Tom!*"

There was a slight noise behind her and she turned just in time to seize a small boy by the slack of his roundabout. "There! I might 'a' thought of that closet. What you been doing in there?"

"Nothing."

"Nothing! Look at your hands. And your mouth. What *is* that truck?"

"*I* don't know, Aunt."

"Well, *I* know. It's jam. Forty times I've said if you didn't let that jam alone I'd skin you. Hand me that switch."

The switch hovered in the air—the peril was desperate—

"My! Look behind you, Aunt!"

The old lady whirled round. The lad fled, on the instant, scrambled up the high board fence and disappeared over it. His Aunt Polly stood surprised a moment, and then broke into a laugh.

"Hang the boy, can't I never learn anything? Ain't he played me tricks enough like that for me to be looking out for him by this time? But my goodness, he never plays tricks alike, two days, and how is a body to know what's coming? And he 'pears to know that if he can put me off for a minute or make me laugh, it's all down again and I can't hit him a lick. I ain't doing my duty by that boy, and that's the truth. But laws-a-me! He's my own dead sister's boy, and I ain't got the heart to lash him, somehow. Every time I let him off, my conscience does hurt me so, and every time I hit him my old heart 'most breaks. Now he'll play hookey this afternoon, and I'll be obleeged to make him work tomorrow to punish him. It's mighty hard to make him work Saturdays, but he hates work more than he hates anything else, and I've *got* to do some of my duty by him or I'll be the ruination of the child."

Tom did play hookey, and he had a very good time. He got back home barely in season to help Jim, the small colored boy, split the kindlings before supper—at least he was there in time to tell his adventures to Jim while Jim did three fourths of the work. Tom's younger brother (or rather, half brother), Sid, was already through with his part of the work (picking up chips), for he was a quiet boy, and had no adventurous, troublesome ways.

While Tom was eating his supper, Aunt Polly asked him questions that were full of guile, and very deep—for she wanted to trap him into damaging revealments. Said she:

"Tom, it was powerful warm in school today, warn't it?"

"Yes'm."

"Didn't you want to go in a-swimming, Tom?"

A bit of a scare shot through Tom—a touch of uncomfortable suspicion. He searched Aunt Polly's face, but it told him nothing. So he said, "No'm—well, not very much."

The old lady reached out and felt Tom's shirt, and said, "But you ain't too warm now, though." It flattered her to reflect that she had discovered that the shirt was dry without anybody knowing that that was what she had in her mind. But in spite of her, Tom knew where the wind lay, now. So he forestalled what might be the next move:

"Some of us pumped on our heads—mine's damp yet. See?"

Aunt Polly was vexed to think she had overlooked that bit of circumstantial evidence. Then she had a new inspiration: "Tom, you didn't have to undo your shirt collar where I sewed it, to pump on your head, did you? Unbutton your jacket!"

The trouble vanished out of Tom's face. He opened his jacket. His shirt collar was securely sewed.

"Bother! Well, go 'long with you. I'd made sure you'd played hookey and been a-swimming. But I forgive ye, Tom. I reckon you're a kind of a singed cat, as the saying is—better'n you look. *This* time." She was half sorry her sagacity had miscarried, and half glad that Tom had stumbled into obedient conduct for once.

But Sidney said, "Well, now, if I didn't think you sewed his collar with white thread, but it's black."

"Why, I did sew it with white! Tom!"

But Tom did not wait for the rest. As he went out at the door he said, "Siddy, I'll lick you for that."

In a safe place Tom examined two large needles which were thrust into the lapels of his jacket, and had thread bound about them—one needle carried white thread and the other black. He said, "She'd never noticed if it hadn't been for Sid. Confound it! Sometimes she sews it with white, and sometimes with black. I wish to geeminy she'd stick to one or t'other—*I* can't keep the run of 'em. But I'll lam Sid for that. I'll learn him!"

Within two minutes, or even less, he had forgotten all his

troubles. Not because his troubles were one whit less heavy and bitter to him than a man's are to a man, but because a powerful new interest bore them down and drove them out of his mind for the time—just as men's misfortunes are forgotten in the excitement of new enterprises. This new interest was a valued novelty in whistling, which he had just acquired and was suffering to practice. It consisted in a peculiar birdlike turn, a sort of liquid warble, produced by touching the tongue to the roof of the mouth at short intervals. Diligence and attention soon gave him the knack of it, and he strode down the street with his mouth full of harmony.

The summer evenings were long. It was not dark, yet. Presently Tom checked his whistle. A stranger was before him—a boy a shade larger than himself. A newcomer of any age or either sex was an impressive curiosity in the poor little village of St. Petersburg. This boy was well dressed, too—well dressed on a weekday. This was simply astounding. His cap was a dainty thing, and his close-buttoned blue cloth roundabout was new and natty. He had shoes on—and it was only Friday. He had a citified air about him that ate into Tom's vitals. The more Tom stared at the splendid marvel, the higher he turned up his nose at his finery and the shabbier and shabbier his own outfit seemed to him to grow. Neither boy spoke. If one moved, the other moved—but only sidewise, in a circle; they kept face to face and eye to eye all the time. Finally Tom said, "I can lick you!"

"I'd like to see you try it."

"Well, I can do it."

"No you can't, either."

"Yes I can."

"You can't."

"Can!"

"Can't!"

An uncomfortable pause. Then Tom said, "What's your name?"

" 'Tisn't any of your business."

"Well I 'low I'll *make* it my business."

"Well why don't you?"

"If you say much, I will."

"Much—much—*much*. There now."

"Oh, you think you're mighty smart, *don't* you? Smarty! Oh, what a hat!"

"You can lump that hat if you don't like it."

"By jingo! For two cents I'd lick you till you couldn't stand up."

The new boy took two coppers out of his pocket and held them out with derision. Tom struck them to the ground. In an instant both boys were rolling and tumbling in the dirt, gripped together like cats, and for the space of a minute they tugged and tore at each other's hair and clothes, punched and scratched each other's noses, and covered themselves with dust and glory. Presently the confusion took form, and through the fog of battle Tom appeared, seated astride the new boy, and pounding him with his fists.

"Holler 'nuff!" said he.

The boy only struggled to free himself. He was crying—mainly from rage.

"Holler 'nuff!"—and the pounding went on.

At last he got out a smothered "'Nuff!" and Tom let him up and said, "Now that'll learn you. Better look out who you're fooling with next time."

The new boy went off, snuffling, and occasionally looking back and threatening what he would do to Tom "next time." To which Tom responded with jeers. As soon as his back was turned the new boy snatched up a stone, threw it and hit him between the shoulders and then turned tail and ran like an antelope. Tom chased the traitor home, and thus found out where he lived. He then held a position at the gate for some time, daring the enemy to come outside, but the enemy only made faces at him through the window. At last the enemy's mother appeared, and called Tom a bad, vicious, vulgar child and ordered him away. So he went away, but he "'lowed" to "lay" for that boy.

He got home pretty late that night, and when he climbed cautiously in at the window, he uncovered an ambuscade in the person of his aunt; and when she saw the state his clothes were in her resolution to turn his Saturday holiday into captivity at hard labor became adamantine in its firmness.

CHAPTER II

SATURDAY MORNING WAS COME, and all the summer world was bright and fresh. There was a song in every heart; and if the heart was young the music issued at the lips. There was cheer in every face and a spring in every step. The locust trees were in bloom and their fragrance filled the air. Cardiff Hill, beyond the village and above it, was green with vegetation and seemed a Delectable Land, dreamy, reposeful and inviting.

Tom appeared on the sidewalk with a bucket of whitewash and a long-handled brush. He surveyed the fence, and all gladness left him. Thirty yards of board fence nine feet high. Life seemed hollow, existence but a burden. Sighing, he dipped his brush and passed it along the top; repeated the operation; did it again; compared the insignificant whitewashed streak with the far-reaching continent of unwhitewashed fence, and sat down on a tree box discouraged. Jim came skipping out at the gate with a tin pail, singing "Buffalo Gals." Bringing water from the town pump had always been hateful work in Tom's eyes, before, but now he remembered that there was company at the pump. Boys and girls were always there waiting their turns, trading playthings, quarreling, skylarking. And he remembered that although the pump was only a hundred and fifty yards off, Jim never got back with a bucket of water under an hour. Tom said:

"Say, Jim, I'll fetch the water if you'll whitewash some."

Jim shook his head and said, "Can't, Marse Tom. Ole Missis, she say she spec' Marse Tom gwine to ax me to whitewash, an' so she tole me go 'long an' 'tend to my own business."

"Oh, never you mind what she said, Jim. Gimme the bucket—*She* won't ever know."

"Oh, I dasn't, Marse Tom."

"Jim, I'll give you a marvel. I'll give you a white alley!"

Jim began to waver.

"White alley, Jim! And it's a bully taw."

"My! Dat's a mighty gay marvel, *I* tell you! But Marse Tom—"

"And besides, if you will I'll show you my sore toe."

Jim was only human—this attraction was too much for him. He put down his pail and bent over the toe with interest while the bandage was being unwound. In another moment he was flying down the street with his pail and a tingling rear, Tom was whitewashing with vigor and Aunt Polly was retiring from the field with a slipper in her hand and triumph in her eye.

But Tom's energy did not last. He began to think of the fun he had planned for this day, and his sorrows multiplied. Soon the free boys would come tripping along on all sorts of delicious expeditions, and they would make a world of fun of him for having to work. He got out his worldly wealth and examined it—bits of toys, marbles and trash; enough to buy an exchange of *work*, maybe, but not half enough to buy so much as half an hour of pure freedom. So he returned his straitened means to his pocket, and gave up the idea of trying to buy the boys. At this dark moment a magnificent inspiration burst upon him!

He took up his brush and went tranquilly to work. Ben Rogers hove in sight presently—the very boy, of all boys, whose ridicule he had been dreading. Ben's gait was the hop-skip-and-jump—proof enough that his heart was light and his anticipations high. He was eating an apple, and giving a long, melodious whoop, at intervals, followed by a deep-toned ding-dong-dong, ding-dong-dong, for he was personating a steamboat. As he drew near he slackened speed, took the middle of the street, leaned far over to starboard and rounded to ponderously—for he was personating the *Big Missouri*, and considered himself to be drawing nine feet of water. He was boat and captain and engine bells combined, so he had to imagine himself standing on his own hurricane deck giving the orders and executing them:

"Stop her, sir! Ting-a-ling-ling! Ship up to back! Ting-a-ling-ling! Set her back on the stabboard! Ting-a-ling-ling! Chow! Ch-chow-wow! Chow!" His right hand, meantime, describing stately circles.

Tom went on whitewashing—paid no attention to the steamboat. Ben stared a moment and then said, "Hi-*yi! You're* up a stump, ain't you!"

No answer. Tom surveyed his last touch with the eye of an artist, then he gave his brush another gentle sweep and surveyed the result, as before. Ben ranged up alongside of him. Tom's mouth watered for the apple, but he stuck to his work. Ben said, "Say—*I'm* going in a-swimming, *I* am. Don't you wish you could? But of course you'd druther *work*—wouldn't you?"

Tom contemplated the boy a bit, and said, "What do you call work?"

"Why, ain't *that* work?"

Tom resumed his whitewashing and answered carelessly, "Well, maybe it is, and maybe it ain't. All I know is, it suits Tom Sawyer."

"Oh come, now, you don't mean to let on that you *like* it?"

The brush continued to move.

"Like it? Well, I don't see why I oughtn't to like it. Does a boy get a chance to whitewash a fence every day?"

That put the thing in a new light. Ben stopped nibbling his apple. Tom swept his brush daintily back and forth—stepped back to note the effect—added a touch here and there—criticized the effect again—Ben watching every move. Presently he said, "Say, Tom, let *me* whitewash a little."

Tom considered. "No—no—I reckon it wouldn't hardly do, Ben. You see, Aunt Polly's awful particular about this fence—right here on the street, you know— It's got to be done very careful. I reckon there ain't one boy in a thousand can do this fence the way it's got to be done."

"Oh come, now—I'd let *you*, if you was me."

"Ben, I'd like to, honest injun; but Aunt Polly—well, Jim wanted to do it, but she wouldn't let him; Sid wanted to do it, and she wouldn't let Sid. If you was to tackle this fence and anything was to happen to it—"

"Oh, shucks, I'll be just as careful. Now lemme try. Say—I'll give you the core of my apple."

"Well, here— No, Ben, I'm afeard—"

"I'll give you *all* of it!"

Tom gave up the brush with reluctance in his face, but alacrity in his heart. And while the late steamer *Big Missouri* worked and sweated in the sun, the retired artist sat on a barrel in the shade close by, dangled his legs, munched his apple and planned the slaughter of more innocents. There was no lack of material; boys happened along every little while; they came to jeer, but remained to whitewash. By the time Ben was fagged out, Tom had traded the next chance to Billy Fisher for a kite; and when *he* played out, Johnny Miller bought in for a dead rat and a string to swing it with—and so on. And when the middle of the afternoon came, from being a poverty-stricken boy in the morning, Tom was literally rolling in wealth. He had, beside the things before mentioned, twelve marbles, part of a Jew's harp, a fragment of chalk, a glass stopper of a decanter, a tin soldier, a kitten with one eye, a brass doorknob, a dog collar—but no dog—four pieces of orange peel and a dilapidated old window sash. He had had a nice, good, idle time all the while—plenty of company—and the fence had three coats of whitewash on it! If he hadn't run out of whitewash, he would have bankrupted every boy in the village.

Tom had discovered a great law of human action, without knowing it—namely, that in order to make a man or a boy covet a thing, it is only necessary to make the thing difficult to attain. If he had been a great philosopher, like the writer of this book, he would have comprehended that Work consists of whatever a body is *obliged* to do, and that Play consists of whatever a body is not obliged to do. And this would help him to understand why constructing artificial flowers or performing on a treadmill is work, while rolling tenpins or climbing Mont Blanc is only amusement.

The boy mused awhile over the substantial change which had taken place in his worldly circumstances, and then wended toward headquarters to report. Aunt Polly was knitting by an open window in a pleasant rearward apartment, which was bedroom, breakfast room, dining room and library combined. She had thought that of course Tom had deserted long ago, and she wondered at seeing him place himself in her power again in this intrepid way. He said, "Mayn't I go and play now, Aunt?"

"What, a'ready? How much have you done?"

"It's all done, Aunt."

"Tom, don't lie to me—I can't bear it."

"I ain't, Aunt; it *is* all done."

Aunt Polly went out to see for herself; and she would have been content to find twenty percent of Tom's statement true. When she found the entire fence not only whitewashed but elaborately coated and recoated, her astonishment was almost unspeakable. She said, "Well, I never! There's no getting round it, you *can* work when you're a mind to, Tom. Well, go 'long and play; but mind you get back sometime in a week, or I'll tan you."

She was so overcome by the splendor of his achievement that she took him into the closet and selected a choice apple and delivered it to him, along with an improving lecture upon the added value and flavor a treat took to itself when it came through virtuous effort. And while she closed with a happy scriptural flourish, he "hooked" a doughnut. Then he skipped out over the fence and was gone. There was a gate, but as a general thing he was too crowded for time to make use of it.

Skirting the block, Tom hastened toward the public square of the village, where two "military" companies of boys had met for conflict, according to appointment. Tom was General of one of these armies, Joe Harper (a bosom friend) General of the other. These two great commanders did not condescend to fight in person, but sat together on an eminence and conducted the field operations by orders delivered through aides-de-camp. Tom's army won a great victory, after a hard-fought battle. Then the dead were counted, prisoners exchanged, the terms of the next disagreement agreed upon and the day for battle appointed; after which the armies marched away, and Tom turned homeward alone.

As he was passing by the house where Jeff Thatcher lived, he saw a new girl in the garden—a lovely little blue-eyed creature with yellow hair plaited into two long tails, white summer frock and embroidered pantalets. The fresh-crowned hero fell without firing a shot. A certain Amy Lawrence vanished out of his heart and left not even a memory of herself behind. He had regarded his passion for Amy as adoration; he had been months winning her; he had been the proudest boy in the world only seven short days, and here in one instant of time she had gone out of his heart like a casual stranger whose visit is done.

He worshiped this new angel with furtive eye, till he saw that she had discovered him; then he pretended he did not know she was present, and began to "show off" in all sorts of absurd ways, in order to win her admiration. While he was in the midst of some dangerous gymnastic performances, he saw that the little girl was wending her way toward the house. Tom came up to the fence and leaned on it, grieving. But his face lit up, right away, for she tossed a pansy over the fence a moment before she disappeared.

The boy ran around and stopped within a foot of the flower, and then shaded his eyes with his hand and began to look down the street as if he had discovered something of interest going on in that direction. Presently he began trying to balance a straw on his nose, with his head tilted far back; and as he moved from side to side, in his efforts, he edged nearer and nearer to the pansy; finally his bare foot rested upon it, his pliant toes closed upon it, and he hopped away with the treasure and disappeared round the corner. There he buttoned the flower inside his jacket, next his heart—or next his stomach, possibly, for he was not much posted in anatomy, and not hypercritical, anyway.

Finally he returned home, with his head full of visions. All through supper his spirits were so high that his aunt wondered "what had got into the child." He tried to steal sugar under his aunt's very nose, and got his knuckles rapped for it. He said, "Aunt, you don't whack Sid when he takes it."

"Well, Sid don't torment a body the way you do."

Presently she stepped into the kitchen, and Sid, happy in his immunity, reached for the sugar bowl—a sort of glorying over Tom which was well-nigh unbearable. But Sid's fingers slipped and the bowl dropped and broke. Tom was in ecstasies, but he controlled his tongue and was silent. He said to himself that even when his aunt came in he would sit perfectly still till she asked who did it; and then he would tell, and see that pet model "catch it." He was full of exultation when the old lady came back and stood above the wreck discharging lightnings of wrath. He said to himself, Now it's coming! And the next instant he was sprawling on the floor! The potent palm was uplifted to strike again when Tom cried out, "Hold on, now, what're you belting *me* for? Sid broke it!"

Aunt Polly paused, perplexed, and Tom looked for healing pity. But when she got her tongue again, she only said, "Umf! Well, you didn't get a lick amiss, I reckon. You been into some other audacious mischief when I wasn't around, like enough."

Then her conscience reproached her, and she yearned to say something kind and loving; but she judged that this would be construed into a confession that she had been in the wrong, and discipline forbade that. So she kept silence, and went about her affairs with a troubled heart. Tom sulked in a corner and exalted his woes. He knew that in her heart his aunt was on her knees to him, and he was morosely gratified. He knew that a yearning glance fell upon him, now and then, through a film of tears, but he refused recognition of it. He pictured himself lying sick unto death and his aunt bending over him beseeching one little forgiving word, but he would turn his face to the wall, and die with that word unsaid. Ah, how would she feel then? And he pictured himself brought home from the river, dead, with his curls all wet, and his sore heart at rest. How she would throw herself upon him, and how her tears would fall like rain, and her lips pray God to give her back her boy! And such a luxury to him was this petting of his sorrows, that he could not bear to have any worldly cheeriness intrude upon it; it was too sacred for such contact; and so, presently, when his cousin Mary danced in, all alive with the joy of seeing home again after an agelong visit of one week to the country, he got up and moved in clouds and darkness out at one door as she brought song and sunshine in at the other.

He wandered far from the accustomed haunts of boys, and sought desolate places in harmony with his spirit. A log raft in the river invited him, and he seated himself on its edge and contemplated the dreary vastness of the stream, wishing he could be drowned, all at once and unconsciously, without undergoing the uncomfortable routine devised by nature. Then he got out his flower, rumpled and wilted, and wondered if *she* would pity him if she knew? At last he rose up sighing and departed in the darkness.

About ten o'clock he came along the deserted street to where the Adored Unknown lived. A candle was casting a dull glow upon the curtain of a second-story window. Was the sacred presence there? He climbed the fence, threaded his stealthy way through the plants, till he stood under that window; he looked up at it with emotion; then he laid him down on the ground under it, disposing himself upon his back, with his hands clasped upon his breast and holding his poor wilted flower. And thus he would die—with no shelter over his homeless head, no loving face to bend pityingly over him when the great agony came! And thus *she* would see him when she looked out upon the glad morning!

The window went up, a maidservant's discordant voice profaned the holy calm, and a deluge of water drenched the martyr's remains! The strangling hero sprang up with a relieving snort. There was a whiz as of a missile in the air, mingled with the murmur of a curse, a sound as of shivering glass followed, and a small, vague form went over the fence and shot away in the gloom.

CHAPTER III

THE SUNDAY SUN ROSE upon a tranquil world and beamed down upon the village like a benediction. Breakfast over, Aunt Polly had family worship; it began with a prayer built from the ground up of solid courses of scriptural quotations, welded together with a thin mortar of originality; and from the summit of this she delivered a grim chapter of the Mosaic law, as from Sinai.

Then Tom girded up his loins, so to speak, and went to work to "get his verses." Sid had learned his lesson days before. Tom bent all his energies to the memorizing of five verses, and he chose part of the Sermon on the Mount, because he could find no verses that were shorter. At the end of half an hour he had a vague general idea of his lesson, but no more, for his mind was traversing the whole field of human thought, and his hands were busy with distracting recreations. Mary took his book to hear him recite, and he tried to find his way through the fog:

"Blessed are the—a—a—"

"Poor—"

"Yes—poor. Blessed are the poor—a—a—"

"In spirit—"

"In spirit. Blessed are the poor in spirit, for they—they—"

"*Theirs*—"

"For *theirs*. Blessed are the poor in spirit, for *theirs* is the kingdom of heaven. Blessed are they that mourn, for they—they—"

"S, h, a—"

"For they s, h— Oh, I don't know what it is!"

"*Shall!*"

"Oh, *shall!* For they shall—a—a—shall *what?* Why don't you tell me, Mary?"

"Oh, Tom, you poor thickheaded thing, you must go learn it again. Don't be discouraged, Tom, you'll manage it—and if you do, I'll give you something nice."

"All right! What is it, Mary? Tell me what it is."

"Never you mind, Tom. You know if I say it's nice, it *is* nice."

"You bet you that's so, Mary. All right, I'll tackle it again."

And he did "tackle it again"—and under the double pressure of curiosity and prospective gain, he did it with such spirit that he accomplished a shining success. Mary gave him a brand-new Barlow knife worth twelve and a half cents; and the delight that swept his system shook him to his foundations. True, the knife would not cut, but it was a "sure enough" Barlow, and Tom contrived to scarify the cupboard with it, and was arranging to begin on the bureau, when he was called off to dress for Sunday school.

Mary gave him a tin basin of water and a piece of soap, and he went outside with it. Then Mary got out a suit of his clothing that had been used only on Sundays during two years—they were simply called his "other clothes"—and so by that we know the size of his wardrobe. The girl "put him to rights" after he had more or less washed and dressed himself; she buttoned his roundabout up to his chin, turned his vast shirt collar down over his shoulders, brushed him off and crowned him with his speckled straw hat. He now looked exceedingly improved and uncomfortable. He hoped that Mary would forget his shoes, but the hope was blighted; she brought them out. He lost his temper and said he was always being made to do everything he didn't want to do. But Mary said, persuasively, "Please, Tom—that's a good boy."

So he got into the shoes, snarling. Mary was soon ready, and the three children set out for Sunday school—a place that Tom hated with his whole heart; but Sid and Mary were fond of it. Sunday school was from nine to half past ten; and then church service.

The church was a small, plain affair, with a sort of pine-board tree box on top of it for a steeple. At the door Tom dropped back a step and accosted a comrade. "Say, Billy, got a yaller ticket?"

"Yes."

"What'll you take for her?"

"What'll you give?"

"Piece of lickrish and a fishhook."

"Let's see 'em."

Tom exhibited. They were satisfactory, and the property changed hands. Then Tom traded a couple of white alleys for three red tickets, and some small trifle or other for a couple of blue ones. He waylaid other boys as they came, and went on buying tickets of various colors ten or fifteen minutes longer. He entered the church, now, with a swarm of clean and noisy boys and girls, proceeded to his seat and started a quarrel with the first boy that came handy. The teacher, a grave, elderly man, interfered; then turned his back a moment and Tom pulled a boy's hair in the next bench. Tom's whole class were of a pattern—restless, noisy, and troublesome.

When they came to recite their lessons, not one of them knew his verses perfectly. However, they worried through, and each got his reward—in small blue tickets, each with a passage of Scripture on it; each blue ticket was pay for two verses of the recitation. Ten blue tickets equaled a red one, ten red tickets equaled a yellow one; for ten yellow tickets the superintendent gave a very plainly bound Bible (worth forty cents in those times) to the pupil. Only the older pupils managed to keep their tickets and stick to their tedious work long enough to get a Bible, and the successful pupil was so conspicuous for that day that every scholar's heart was fired with a fresh ambition that often lasted a couple of weeks. It is possible that Tom's mental stomach had never really hungered for one of those prizes, but unquestionably his entire being had for many a day longed for the glory that came with it.

In due course the superintendent stood up in front of the pulpit and commanded attention. This superintendent, Mr. Walters, was a slim creature of thirty-five, with a sandy goatee and short sandy hair; and he wore a stiff standing collar whose upper edge almost reached his ears. He was very earnest of mien, and he held sacred things in such reverence, and so separated them from worldly matters, that unconsciously to himself his Sunday-school voice had acquired a peculiar intonation which was wholly absent on week-days. He began after this fashion:

"Now, children, I want you all to sit up just as straight and pretty as you can and give me all your attention. I see one little girl who is looking out of the window—I am afraid she thinks I am out there somewhere—perhaps up in one of the trees making a speech to the little birds. [Applausive titter.] I want to tell you how good it makes me feel to see so many bright, clean little faces assembled in a place like this, learning to do right and be good." And so forth and so on. The latter third of the speech was marred by the resumption of fights and other recreations among certain of the bad boys, and by fidgetings and whisperings that extended far and wide, washing even to the bases of isolated and incorruptible rocks like Sid and Mary. But now every sound ceased suddenly, with the subsidence of Mr. Walters' voice, and the conclusion of the speech was received with a burst of silent gratitude.

A good part of the whispering had been occasioned by the entrance of visitors: Lawyer Thatcher with a portly, middle-aged gentleman with iron-gray hair, and a dignified lady who was doubtless the latter's wife. The lady was leading a child. When Tom saw this small newcomer his soul was at once ablaze with bliss. The next moment he was "showing off" with all his might—cuffing boys, pulling hair, making faces—in a word, using every art that seemed likely to fascinate a girl and win her applause.

The visitors were given the highest seat of honor, and Mr. Walters introduced them to the school. The middle-aged man turned out to be no less than the County Judge—altogether the most august creation these children had ever looked upon. He was from Constantinople, twelve miles away—so he had traveled, and seen the world—these very eyes had looked upon the county courthouse, which was said to have a tin roof. The awe which these reflections inspired was attested by the ranks of staring eyes. This was the great Judge Thatcher, brother of their own lawyer, who was Jeff Thatcher's father. Jeff Thatcher immediately went forward, to be familiar with the great man and be envied by the school. It would have been music to his soul to hear the whisperings:

"Look at him, Jim! He's a-going up there. Say! By jings, don't you wish you was Jeff?"

Mr. Walters fell to "showing off" with all sorts of official bustlings and activities, giving orders, delivering judgments, discharging directions here, there, everywhere. The librarian "showed off"—running hither and thither with his arms full of books. The young lady teachers "showed off"—bending sweetly over pupils that were lately being boxed—and the little boys "showed off" with such diligence that the air was thick with paper wads and the murmur of scufflings. And above it all the great man beamed a majestic smile upon all the house, and warmed himself in the sun of his own grandeur—for he was "showing off," too.

There was only one thing wanting to make Mr. Walters' ecstasy complete, and that was a chance to deliver a Bible prize and exhibit a prodigy. Several pupils had a few tickets, but none had enough.

And now at this moment, when hope was dead, Tom Sawyer came forward with nine yellow tickets, nine red tickets and ten blue ones, and demanded a Bible. This was a thunderbolt out of a clear sky. Walters was not expecting an application from this source for the next ten years. But there was no getting around it—here were the certified checks. Tom was therefore elevated to a place with the Judge and the other elect, and the great news was announced. It was the most stunning surprise of the decade. The boys were all eaten up with envy—but those that suffered the bitterest pangs were those who perceived that they themselves had contributed to this hated splendor by trading tickets to Tom for the wealth he had amassed in selling whitewashing privileges.

The prize was delivered to Tom with as much effusion as the superintendent could pump up under the circumstances; but it lacked the true gush, for the poor fellow's instinct taught him that there was a mystery here that could not well bear the light. Tom was then introduced to the Judge; but his tongue was tied, his heart quaked—partly because of the awful greatness of the man, but mainly because he was *her* parent. The Judge put his hand on Tom's head and called him a fine little man, and asked him what his name was. The boy stammered, gasped, and got it out:

"Tom."

"Oh, no, not Tom—it is—"

"Thomas."

"Ah, that's it. But you've another one I daresay."

"Tell the gentleman your other name, Thomas," said Walters, "and say *sir*. You mustn't forget your manners."

"Thomas Sawyer—sir."

"That's a good boy. Fine, manly little fellow. Two thousand verses is a great many—very, very great many. And you never can be sorry for the trouble you took to learn them; for knowledge is worth more than anything in the world; it's what makes great men and good men; you'll be a great man and a good man yourself, someday, Thomas, and then you'll look back and say, 'It's all owing to the precious Sunday-school privileges of my boyhood!' And now, Thomas, you wouldn't mind telling me and this lady some of the things you've learned, for we are proud of little boys that learn. Now, no doubt you know the names of the twelve disciples. Won't you tell us the names of the first two that were appointed?"

Tom was tugging at a buttonhole. He blushed, and his eyes fell. Mr. Walters' heart sank within him. Yet he felt obliged to speak up and say, "Answer the gentleman, Thomas—don't be afraid."

Tom still hung fire.

"Now I know you'll tell *me*," said the lady. "The names of the first two disciples were—"

"DAVID AND GOLIATH!"

Let us draw the curtain of charity over the rest of the scene.

ABOUT HALF PAST TEN the cracked bell of the small church rang, and the people began to gather for the sermon. The Sunday-school children distributed themselves about the house and occupied pews with their parents, so as to be under supervision. Aunt Polly came, and Tom and Sid and Mary sat with her—Tom being placed next the aisle, in order that he might be as far away from the open window and the seductive outside scenes as possible. The crowd filed up the aisles: the aged postmaster; the mayor and his wife; the justice of the peace; the Widow Douglas, fair, smart and forty, a good-hearted soul and well-to-do, her hill mansion the only palace in the town, and the most hospitable in the matter of festivities that St. Petersburg could boast; then, all the young clerks in town in a body—for they had stood in the vestibule, sucking their cane heads, till the last girl had run their gantlet.

The congregation being fully assembled, the bell rang once more, and a solemn hush fell upon the church. The minister gave out the hymn, and after it had been sung, he turned himself into a bulletin board, and read off "notices." And now he prayed. A good, generous prayer it was: it pleaded for the church, and the little children of the church; for the other churches of the village; for the village itself; for the county, the state, the state officers, the United States, the churches of the United States, Congress, the President; for poor sailors, tossed by stormy seas; for oppressed millions groaning under the heel of despotisms; for such as have the light and the good tidings, and yet have not eyes to see nor ears to hear withal; for the heathen in the far islands of the sea; and closed with a supplication that the words he was about to speak might find grace and favor, and be as seed sown in fertile ground, yielding in time a grateful harvest of good. Amen.

The boy whose history this book relates was restive all through the prayer, for he was not listening, but knew the ground of old.

In the midst of it a fly had lit on the pew in front of him and tortured his spirit by calmly rubbing its hands together, embracing its head with its arms, and polishing it so vigorously that it seemed to almost part company with the body; scraping its wings with its hind legs and smoothing them as if they had been coattails; going through its whole toilet as tranquilly as if it knew it was perfectly safe. As indeed it was; for as sorely as Tom's hands itched to grab for it they did not dare—he believed his soul would be instantly destroyed if he did such a thing while the prayer was going on. But with the closing sentence his hand began to steal forward; and the instant the "Amen" was out the fly was a prisoner of war. His aunt detected the act and made him let it go.

The minister gave out his text and droned along. Tom counted the pages of the sermon; after church he always knew how many pages there had been, but he seldom knew anything else about it. Presently he bethought him of a treasure he had and got it out. It was a large black beetle with formidable jaws—a "pinch bug," he called it. It was in a percussion-cap box. The first thing the beetle did was to take him by the finger. A natural fillip followed, the beetle went flying into the aisle and lit on its back, and the hurt finger went into the boy's mouth. The beetle lay there working its helpless legs, unable to turn over. Tom eyed it, and longed for it; but it was safe out of his reach. Other people, uninterested in the sermon, found relief in the beetle, and they eyed it too.

Presently a vagrant poodle dog came idling along, sad at heart, sighing for change. He spied the beetle; the drooping tail lifted and wagged. He surveyed the prize; walked around it; smelled at it from a safe distance; walked around it again; grew bolder, and took a closer smell; then lifted his lip and made a gingerly snatch at it, just missing it; made another; subsided to his stomach with the beetle between his paws, and continued his experiments; grew weary at last, and then indifferent. For a time he followed an ant around, with his nose close to the floor, and wearied of that; yawned, forgot the beetle entirely, and sat down on it. Then there was a wild yelp of agony and the poodle dog went sailing up the aisle; he crossed the house in front of the altar; he flew down the other aisle; his anguish grew with his progress, till he was but a woolly comet moving in its orbit with the speed of light. At last the frantic sufferer sheered from its course, and sprang into its master's lap; his master flung it out of the window, and the voice of distress quickly died in the distance.

By this time the whole church was red-faced and suffocating with suppressed laughter, and the sermon had come to a dead standstill. It was resumed presently, but it went lame and halting, for even the gravest sentiments were received with a smothered burst of unholy mirth. It was a genuine relief to the whole congregation when the ordeal was over and the benediction pronounced.

Tom Sawyer went home quite cheerful, thinking to himself that there was some satisfaction about divine service when there was a bit of variety in it. He had but one marring thought; he was willing that the dog should play with his pinch bug, but he did not think it was upright in him to carry it off.

CHAPTER IV

MONDAY MORNING FOUND Tom Sawyer miserable. Monday morning always found him so—because it began another week's slow suffering in school. He generally began that day with wishing he had had no intervening holiday, it made the going into captivity again so much more odious.

Tom lay thinking. Presently it occurred to him that he wished he was sick; then he could stay home from school. He canvassed his system. No ailment was found, and he investigated again. Suddenly he discovered something. One of his upper front teeth was loose. But when he went downstairs and complained that the tooth ached, his aunt called Mary. "Mary, get me a silk thread, and a chunk of fire out of the kitchen stove."

Tom said, "Oh, Auntie, don't pull it out. It don't hurt anymore. Please don't, Auntie. *I* don't want to stay home from school."

"Oh, you don't, don't you? So all this row was because you thought you'd get to stay home from school?" By this time the dental instruments were ready. The old lady made one end of the thread fast to Tom's tooth with a loop and tied the other to the bedpost. Then she seized the chunk of fire and suddenly thrust it almost into the boy's face. The tooth hung dangling by the bedpost.

But all trials bring their compensations. As Tom wended to school he was the envy of every boy he met because the gap in his teeth enabled him to expectorate in a new and admirable way; he gathered quite a following of lads interested in the exhibition.

Shortly Tom came upon the juvenile pariah of the village, Huckleberry Finn, son of the town drunkard. Huckleberry was cordially hated and dreaded by all the mothers of the town, because he was idle and lawless and vulgar and bad—and because all their children admired him so, and delighted in his forbidden society. Tom envied Huckleberry his gaudy outcast condition, and was under strict orders not to play with him. So he played with him every time he got the chance.

Huckleberry was always dressed in the cast-off clothes of full-grown men. His hat was a vast ruin with a wide crescent lopped out of its brim; his coat, when he wore one, hung nearly to his heels, and but one suspender supported his trousers. Huckleberry came and went at his own free will. He slept on doorsteps in fine weather and in empty hogsheads in wet; he did not have to go to school or to church; he could go fishing or swimming when and where he chose; he was the first boy that went barefoot in the spring and the last to resume leather in the fall; he never had to wash; he could swear wonderfully. In a word, everything that goes to make life precious, that boy had. So thought every harassed, hampered, respectable boy in St. Petersburg.

Tom hailed the romantic outcast: "Hello, Huckleberry!"

"Hello yourself, and see how you like it."

"What's that you got?"

"Dead cat."

"Lemme see, Huck. He's pretty stiff. Where'd you get him?"

"Bought him off'n a boy."

"What did you give?"

"I give a bladder that I got at the slaughterhouse."

"Say—what is dead cats good for, Huck?"

"Good for? Cure warts with."

"No! Is that so? I know something that's better. Spunkwater."

"Spunkwater! I wouldn't give a dern for spunkwater."

"You wouldn't, wouldn't you? D'you ever try it?"

"No, I hain't. But Bob Tanner did."

"Tell me how Bob Tanner done it, Huck."

"Why, he took and dipped his hand in a rotten stump where the rainwater was."

"In the daytime?"

"Certainly."

"Did he *say* anything?"

"I don't reckon he did. I don't know."

"Aha! Talk about trying to cure warts with spunkwater such a blame-fool way as that! Why, you got to go to the stump at night, and just as it's midnight you back up against the stump and jam your hand in and say,

Barleycorn, Barleycorn, injun-meal shorts,
Spunkwater, spunkwater, swaller these warts,

and then walk away quick, eleven steps, and then turn around three times and walk home without speaking to anybody. Because if you speak the charm's busted."

"Well, that sounds like a good way, but that ain't the way Bob Tanner done."

"No, sir, you can bet he didn't, becuz he's the wartiest boy in this town; and he wouldn't have a wart on him if he'd knowed how to work spunkwater. I've took thousands of warts off that way, Huck. I play with frogs so much that I've always got considerable many warts. But say—how do you cure 'em with dead cats?"

"Why, you take your cat and go in the graveyard 'long about midnight when somebody that was wicked has been buried; and when it's midnight a devil will come, or maybe two or three, but you can't see 'em, you can only hear something like the wind, or maybe hear 'em talk; and when they're taking that feller away, you heave your cat after 'em and say, 'Devil follow corpse, cat follow devil, warts follow cat, *I*'m done with ye!' That'll fetch *any* wart."

"Sounds right. D'you ever try it, Huck?"

"No, but old Mother Hopkins told me."

"Well, I reckon it's so, then. Becuz they say she's a witch."

"Say! Why, Tom, I *know* she is. She witched Pap one day and he rolled off'n a shed wher' he was a-layin' drunk, and broke his arm."

"Why, that's awful. How did he know she witched him?"

"Lord, Pap can tell, easy. Pap says when they keep looking at you right stiddy, they're a-witching you. Specially if they mumble. When they mumble they're saying the Lord's Prayer backwards."

"Say, Hucky, when you going to try the cat?"

"Tonight. I reckon they'll come after old Hoss Williams tonight."

"But they buried him Saturday. Didn't they get him Saturday night?"

"Why, how you talk! How could their charms work till midnight? And *then* it's Sunday. Devils don't slosh around much of a Sunday, I don't reckon."

"I never thought of that. That's so. Lemme go with you?"

"Of course—if you ain't afeard."

"Afeard! 'Tain't likely. Will you meow?"

"Yes—and you meow back. Last time, you kep' me a-meowing around till old Hays went to throwing rocks at me and says 'Dern that cat!' "

"I couldn't meow that night, becuz Auntie was watching me, but I'll meow this time."

The boys separated. When Tom reached the little isolated frame schoolhouse, he strode in briskly, with the manner of one who had come with all honest speed. He hung his hat on a peg and flung himself into his seat with businesslike alacrity. The master, throned on high in his great armchair, was dozing, lulled by the drowsy hum of study. The interruption roused him.

"Thomas Sawyer!"

Tom knew that when his name was pronounced in full, it meant trouble.

"Sir!"

"Come up here. Now, sir, why are you late again, as usual?"

Tom was about to take refuge in a lie, when he saw two long tails of yellow hair hanging down a back that he recognized; and by that form was *the only vacant place* on the girls' side of the schoolhouse. He instantly said:

"I STOPPED TO TALK WITH HUCKLEBERRY FINN!"

The master stared. The buzz of study ceased. The pupils wondered if this foolhardy boy had lost his mind. The master said:

"You—you did what?"

"Stopped to talk with Huckleberry Finn."

"Thomas Sawyer, this is the most astounding confession I have ever listened to. No mere ferule will answer for this offense. Take off your jacket."

The master's arm performed until it was tired. Then the order followed: "Now, sir, go and sit with the *girls!* And let this be a warning to you."

The titter that rippled around the room appeared to abash the boy, but in reality that result was caused rather more by his worshipful awe of his unknown idol. He sat down upon the end of the pine bench, and the girl hitched herself away from him. Nudges and winks and whispers traversed the room, but Tom sat still, with his arms upon the desk before him, and seemed to study his book.

By and by attention ceased from him, and the accustomed school murmur rose once more. Presently the boy began to steal furtive glances at the girl. She observed it, "made a mouth" at him and gave him the back of her head. When she cautiously faced around again, a peach lay before her. She thrust it away. Tom gently put it back. She thrust it away again, but with less animosity. Tom patiently returned it. Then she let it remain. Tom scrawled on his slate, *Please take it—I got more*. The girl glanced at the words, but made no sign. Now the boy began to draw something, hiding his work with his left hand. For a time the girl refused to notice; but her human curiosity presently began to manifest itself. At last she gave in and hesitatingly whispered:

"Let me see it."

Tom uncovered a dismal caricature of a house with two gable

ends and a corkscrew of smoke issuing from the chimney. The girl gazed a moment, then whispered, "It's nice—make a man."

The artist erected a man in the front yard, that resembled a derrick. He could have stepped over the house; but the girl was not hypercritical; she was satisfied with the monster, and whispered, "It's ever so nice—I wish I could draw."

"It's easy," whispered Tom, "I'll learn you."

"Oh, will you? When?"

"At noon. Do you go home to dinner?"

"I'll stay if you will."

"Good—that's a go. What's your name?"

"Becky Thatcher. What's yours? Oh, I know. It's Thomas Sawyer."

"That's the name they lick me by. I'm Tom when I'm good. You call me Tom, will you?"

"Yes."

Now Tom began to scrawl something on the slate, hiding the words from the girl. But she was not backward this time. She begged to see. Tom said, "Oh, it ain't anything."

"Yes it is."

"No it ain't. You don't want to see it."

"Yes I do. Please let me." And she put her small hand upon his and a little scuffle ensued, Tom pretending to resist but letting his hand slip by degrees till these words were revealed: *I love you.*

"Oh, you bad thing!" And she hit his hand a smart rap, but reddened and looked pleased, nevertheless.

Just at this juncture the boy felt a slow, fateful grip closing on his ear, and a steady lifting impulse. In that vise he was borne across the house and deposited in his own seat, under a peppering fire of giggles. Then the master stood over him during a few awful moments, and finally moved away to his throne without saying a word. But although Tom's ear tingled, his heart was jubilant.

As the school quieted down Tom made an honest effort to study, but the turmoil within him was too great. In turn he took his place in the reading class and made a botch of it; then in the geography class and turned lakes into mountains, mountains into rivers and rivers into continents, till chaos was come again; then in the spelling class, and got "turned down," by a succession of mere baby words, till he brought up at the very foot. But at last school broke up at noon. Tom flew to Becky Thatcher, and whispered in her ear.

"Put on your bonnet and let on you're going home; and when you get to the corner, give the rest of 'em the slip and come back. I'll go the other way and come it over 'em the same way."

So the one went off with one group of scholars, and the other with another. In a little while the two met at the bottom of the lane, and when they reached the school they had it all to themselves. Then they sat together, with a slate before them, and Tom gave Becky the pencil and held her hand in his, guiding it, and so created another surprising house. When the interest in art began to wane, the two fell to talking. Tom was swimming in bliss. He said:

"Do you love rats?"

"No! I hate them!"

"Well, I do, too—*live* ones. But I mean dead ones, to swing round your head with a string."

"No, I don't care for rats much, anyway. What *I* like is chewing gum."

"Oh, I should say so. I wish I had some now."

"Do you? I've got some. I'll let you chew it a while, but you must give it back to me."

That was agreeable, so they chewed it turn about, and dangled their legs against the bench in excess of contentment.

"Was you ever at a circus?" said Tom.

"Yes, and my pa's going to take me again, if I'm good."

"I been to the circus three or four times—lots of times. Church ain't shucks to a circus. I'm going to be a clown when I grow up."

"Oh, are you! That will be nice. They're so lovely, all spotted up."

"Yes. And they get slathers of money—'most a dollar a day, Ben Rogers says. Say, Becky, was you ever engaged?"

"What's that?"

"Why, engaged to be married."

"No."

"Would you like to?"

"I reckon so. I don't know. What is it like?"

"Like? Why it ain't like anything. You only just tell a boy you won't ever have anybody but him, ever ever *ever*, and then you kiss and that's all. Anybody can do it."

"Kiss? What do you kiss for?"

"Why, that, you know, is to—well, they always do that."

"Everybody?"

"Why yes, everybody that's in love with each other. Do you remember what I wrote on the slate?"

"Ye—yes."

"What was it?"

"I shan't tell you."

"Shall I tell *you*?"

"Ye—yes—but some other time."

"Oh, no, *now*. Please, Becky—I'll whisper it, ever so easy."

Becky hesitating, Tom took silence for consent, and passed his arm about her waist and whispered the tale ever so softly, with his mouth close to her ear. And then he added, "Now you whisper it to me—just the same."

She resisted, for a while, and then said, "You turn your face away so you can't see, and then I will."

He turned his face away. She bent timidly around till her breath stirred his curls and whispered, "I—love—you!"

Then she sprang away and ran around and around the desks and benches, with Tom after her, and took refuge in a corner at last, with her little white apron to her face. Tom clasped her about her neck and pleaded, "Now, Becky, it's done—all over but the kiss. Don't be afraid of that—it ain't anything at all. Please, Becky." And he tugged at her apron.

By and by she let her hands drop; her face, all glowing with the struggle, came up and submitted. Tom kissed the red lips and said, "Now it's all done, Becky. And always after this, you know, you ain't ever to love anybody but me, and you ain't ever to marry anybody but me, never never and forever. Will you?"

"No, I'll never love anybody but you, Tom, and I'll never marry anybody but you—and you ain't to ever marry anybody but me, either."

"Certainly. Of course. That's *part* of it. And always coming to school, you're to walk with me, when there ain't anybody looking—and you choose me and I choose you at parties, because that's the way you do when you're engaged."

"It's nice. I never heard of it before."

"Oh, it's ever so gay! Why, me and Amy Lawrence—"

The big eyes told Tom his blunder and he stopped, confused.

"Oh, Tom! Then I ain't the first you've ever been engaged to!"

The child began to cry. Tom said, "Oh, don't cry, Becky, I don't care for her anymore."

"Yes, you do, Tom—you know you do."

Tom tried to put his arm about her neck, but she pushed him away and turned her face to the wall, and went on crying. Tom tried again, and was repulsed again. Then his pride was up, and he strode outside. He stood about, restless and uneasy, hoping she would repent and come to find him. But she did not. He finally went back to her and stood a moment, not knowing exactly how to proceed. She was still in the corner, sobbing. Then he said hesitatingly, "Becky, I—I don't care for anybody but you. Becky, won't you say something?"

No reply—but sobs. Tom got out his chiefest jewel, a brass knob from an andiron, and passed it around her so that she could see it, and said:

"Please, Becky, won't you take it?"

She struck it to the floor. Then Tom marched out of the house and over the hills and far away, to return to school no more that day. Presently Becky began to suspect. She ran to the door; he was not in sight; she flew around to the play yard; he was not there. Then she called, "Tom! Come back, Tom!"

She listened intently, but there was no answer. So she sat down to upbraid herself; and by this time the scholars began to gather again, and she had to hide her griefs and take up the cross of a long, dreary afternoon, with none among the strangers about her to exchange sorrows with.

CHAPTER V

At half past nine that night, Tom and Sid were sent to bed as usual. Sid was soon asleep, and Tom lay awake and waited, in restless impatience. When it seemed to him that it must be nearly daylight, he heard the clock strike ten! This was despair. He would have tossed and fidgeted, but he was afraid he might wake Sid. Everything was dismally still. At last he was satisfied that time had ceased and eternity begun; he began to doze, in spite of himself; the clock chimed eleven, but he did not hear it. And then there came, mingling with his half-formed dreams, a most melancholy caterwauling. The raising of a neighboring window disturbed him. A cry of "Scat! you devil!" and the crash of an empty bottle brought him wide awake, and a minute later he was dressed and out the window and creeping along the roof of the "ell." He meowed with caution, then jumped to the roof of the woodshed and thence to the ground. Huckleberry Finn was there, with his dead cat. The boys disappeared in the gloom. At the end of half an hour they were wading through the tall grass of the graveyard.

The graveyard was on a hill about a mile and a half from the village. It had a crazy board fence around it, which leaned inward in places, and outward the rest of the time, but stood upright nowhere. Grass and weeds grew rank. All the old graves were sunken in, and round-topped, worm-eaten boards staggered over them, leaning for support and finding none. "Sacred to the memory of" so-and-so had been painted on them once, but it could no longer have been read on most of them, even if there had been light.

A faint wind moaned through the trees. The boys talked little, for the place oppressed their spirits. They found the sharp new heap they were seeking, and ensconced themselves within the protection of three great trees a few feet from the grave.

They waited for a long time. The hooting of an owl was all that troubled the dead stillness. At last Tom said in a whisper, "Hucky, do you believe the dead people like it for us to be here?"

Huckleberry whispered, "I wisht I knowed. It's awful solemn."

The boys canvassed this matter inwardly. Then Tom whispered, "Say, Hucky—do you reckon Hoss Williams hears us talking?"

"O' course he does. Least his sperrit does."

Tom, after a pause: "I wish I'd said *Mister* Williams. But I never meant any harm. Everybody calls him Hoss."

"A body can't be too particular how they talk 'bout these yer dead people, Tom."

This was a damper, and conversation died again.

Presently Tom seized his comrade's arm and said, "*Sh!*"

"What is it, Tom?" And the two clung together.

"Sh! There 'tis again! Didn't you hear it?"

"Lord, Tom, they're coming, sure! What'll we do?"

"I dono. Think they'll see us?"

"Tom, they can see in the dark, same as cats. I wisht I hadn't come."

"*I* don't believe they'll bother us. We ain't doing any harm. If we keep perfectly still, maybe they won't notice us at all. . . . Listen!"

The boys scarcely breathed. A muffled sound of voices floated up from the far end of the graveyard.

"Look! See there!" whispered Tom. "What is it?"

"It's devil-fire. Oh, Tom, this is awful."

Some vague figures approached through the gloom, swinging an old-fashioned tin lantern that freckled the ground with innumerable little spangles of light. Presently Huckleberry whispered with a shudder, "It's the devils, sure enough. Three of 'em! Lordy, Tom, we're goners! Can you pray?"

"I'll try. 'Now I lay me down to sleep, I—' What is it, Huck?"

"They're *humans!* One of 'em is, anyway. One of 'em's old Muff Potter's voice. Drunk, the same as usual, likely—blamed old rip!"

"Say, Huck, I know another o' them voices; it's Injun Joe."

"That's so—that murderin' half-breed! I'd druther they was devils a dern sight. What kin they be up to?"

The whispers died wholly out, now, for the three men had reached the grave and stood within a few feet of the boys' hiding place.

"Here it is," said the third voice; and the owner of it held the lantern up and revealed the face of young Dr. Robinson.

Potter and Injun Joe were carrying a handbarrow with a rope and a couple of shovels on it. They cast down their load and began to open the grave. The doctor put the lantern at the head of the grave and came and sat down with his back against one of the trees. He was so close the boys could have touched him.

"Hurry, men!" he said in a low voice. "The moon might come out any moment."

They growled a response and went on digging. For some time there was no noise but the grating sound of the spades. It was very monotonous.

Finally a spade struck upon the coffin with a dull woody accent, and within another minute or two the men had hoisted it out. They pried off the lid and dumped the body rudely on the ground. The moon drifted from behind the clouds and exposed the pallid face. The corpse was placed on the barrow, covered with a blanket and bound to its place with the rope.

Potter took out a large spring knife and cut off the dangling end of the rope and then said, "Now the cussed thing's ready, Sawbones, and you'll just out with another five, or here she stays."

"That's the talk!" said Injun Joe.

"Look here, what does this mean?" said the doctor. "You required your pay in advance, and I've paid you."

"Yes, and you done more than that," said Injun Joe, approaching the doctor. "Five years ago you drove me away from your father's kitchen one night, when I asked for something to eat, and you said I warn't there for any good; and when I swore I'd get even with you, your father had me jailed for a vagrant. Did you think I'd forget? The Injun blood ain't in me for nothing. And now I've *got* you, and you got to *settle!*"

He was threatening the doctor, with his fist in his face, by this time. The doctor struck out suddenly and stretched the ruffian on the ground. Potter dropped his knife, and exclaimed:

"Here, now, don't you hit my pard!" and the next moment he had grappled with the doctor and the two were struggling with might and main, trampling the grass and tearing the ground with their heels.

Injun Joe sprang to his feet, his eyes flaming, snatched up Potter's knife and went creeping, catlike and stooping, round and round the combatants, seeking an opportunity. All at once the doctor flung himself free, seized the heavy headboard of Williams' grave and felled Potter with it—and in the same instant the half-breed saw his chance and drove the knife to the hilt in the young man's breast. He reeled and fell partly upon Potter, flooding him with his blood, and in the same moment the clouds blotted out the dreadful spectacle and the two frightened boys went speeding away in the dark.

Presently, when the moon emerged again, Injun Joe was standing over the two forms. The doctor gave a long gasp or two and was still. The half-breed muttered:

"*That* score is settled—damn you."

Then he robbed the body. After which he put the fatal knife in Potter's open right hand, and sat down on the coffin.

Three—four—five minutes passed, and then Potter began to stir and moan. His hand closed upon the knife; he raised it, glanced at it, and let it fall, with a shudder. Then he sat up, pushing the body from him, and gazed at it, and then around him, confusedly. His eyes met Joe's.

"Lord, how is this, Joe?" he said.

"It's a dirty business," said Joe, without moving. "What did you do it for?"

"I! I never done it!"

"Look here! That kind of talk won't wash."

Potter trembled and grew white.

"I thought I'd got sober. I'd no business to drink tonight. But it's in my head yet—worse'n when we started here. I'm all in a muddle; can't recollect anything of it, hardly. Tell me, Joe—*honest*, now, old feller—did I do it? Joe, I never meant to—'pon my soul and honor! Oh, it's awful—and him so young and promising. Joe, don't tell! Say you won't tell, Joe! I always liked you, Joe, and stood up for you. You *won't* tell, *will* you, Joe?" And the poor creature dropped on his knees before the stolid murderer, and clasped his appealing hands.

"No, you've always been fair and square with me, Muff Potter, and I won't go back on you. There, now, that's as fair as a man can say."

"Oh, Joe, I'll bless you for this the longest day I live." And Potter began to cry.

"Come, now, this ain't any time for blubbering. You be off yonder way and I'll go this. Move, now, and don't leave any tracks."

Potter started on a trot that quickly increased to a run. The half-breed stood looking after him. He muttered:

"If he's as much stunned with the lick and fuddled with the rum as he had the look of being, he won't think of the knife till he's gone so far he'll be afraid to come back after it to such a place by himself—chickenheart!"

Two or three minutes later the murdered man, the blanketed corpse, the lidless coffin and the open grave were under no inspection but the moon's.

The stillness was complete again, too.

CHAPTER VI

THE TWO BOYS FLEW ON AND ON, toward the village, speechless with horror. They glanced backward over their shoulders from time to time, apprehensively, as if they feared they might be followed. Every stump that started up in their path seemed a man and an enemy, and made them catch their breath; and as they sped by some outlying cottages near the village, the barking of the aroused watchdogs seemed to give wings to their feet.

"If we can only get to the old tannery before we break down!" whispered Tom, in short catches between breaths. "I can't stand it much longer."

Huckleberry's hard pantings were his only reply. The boys gained steadily on their goal, and at last they burst through the open door of the tannery and fell grateful and exhausted in the sheltering shadows beyond. By and by their pulses slowed down, and Tom whispered:

"Huck, what do you reckon'll come of this?"

"If Dr. Robinson dies, I reckon hanging'll come of it."

"Do you though?"

"Why, I *know* it, Tom."

Tom thought awhile, then he said:

"Who'll tell? We?"

"What are you talking about? S'pose something happened and Injun Joe *didn't* hang? Why he'd kill us some time or other, just as dead sure as we're a-laying here."

"That's just what I was thinking to myself, Huck."

"If anybody tells, let Muff Potter do it, if he's fool enough. He's generally drunk enough."

Tom said nothing—went on thinking. Presently he whispered:

"Huck, Muff Potter don't *know* it. How can he tell?"

"What's the reason he don't know it?"

"Because he'd just got that whack when Injun Joe done it. D'you reckon he could see anything? D'you reckon he knowed anything?"

"By hokey, that's so, Tom!"

"And besides, looky here—maybe that whack done for *him!*"

"No, 'tain't likely, Tom. He had liquor in him; I could see that. But if a man was dead sober, I reckon maybe that whack might fetch him; I dono."

After another reflective silence, Tom said:

"Hucky, you sure you can keep mum?"

"Tom, we *got* to keep mum. *You* know that. That Injun devil wouldn't make any more of drownding us than a couple of cats, if we was to squeak 'bout this and they didn't hang him. Now, looky here, Tom, let's take and swear to one another—that's what we got to do—swear to keep mum."

"I'm agreed. It's the best thing. Would you just hold hands and swear that we—"

"Oh, no, that wouldn't do for this. That's good enough for little rubbishy common things—specially with gals, cuz *they* go back on you anyway, and blab if they get in a huff—but there orter be writing 'bout a big thing like this. And blood."

Tom's whole being applauded this idea. It was deep, and dark, and awful; the hour, the circumstances, the surroundings, were in keeping with it. He picked up a clean pine shingle that lay in the moonlight, took a little fragment of "red keel" out of his pocket, got the moon on his work, and painfully scrawled these lines, emphasizing each slow downstroke by clamping his tongue between his teeth, and letting up the pressure on the upstrokes:

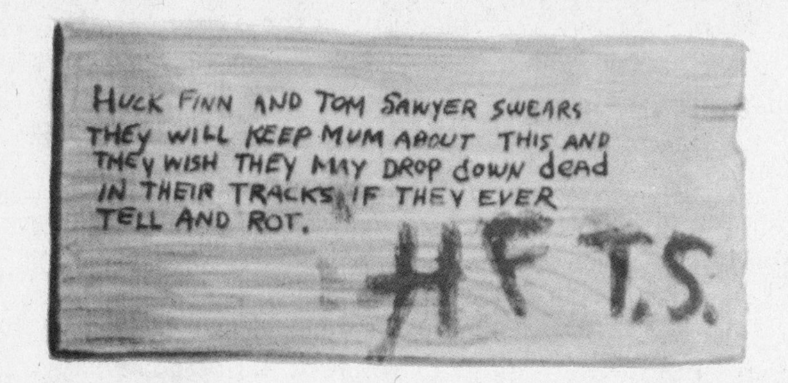

Huckleberry was filled with admiration for the sublimity of Tom's language. He at once took a pin from his lapel, and each boy pricked his thumb and squeezed out a drop of blood. In time, after many squeezes, Tom managed to sign his initials. Then he showed Huckleberry how to make an H and an F, and the oath was complete. They buried the shingle close to the wall, with some dismal incantations, and the fetters that bound their tongues were considered to be locked and the key thrown away.

A figure crept stealthily through a break in the other end of the ruined building, now, but they did not notice it.

"Tom," whispered Huckleberry, "does this keep us from *ever* telling—*always?*"

"Of course it does. We'd drop down dead if we tell—don't *you* know that?"

"Yes, I reckon that's so."

Presently, just outside, a dog set up a long, lugubrious howl. The boys clasped each other suddenly, in an agony of fright.

"Which of us does he mean?" gasped Huckleberry. "Which does he mean is gonna die?"

"I dono—peep through the crack. Quick!"

"No, *you*, Tom!"

"I can't—I can't *do* it, Huck!"

"Please, Tom. Maybe it ain't a stray. There 'tis again!"

Tom, quaking with fear, put his eye to the crack. His whisper was hardly audible when he said, "Oh, Huck, IT IS A STRAY!"

"Quick, Tom, quick! Who does he mean?"

"Huck, he must mean us both—we're right together."

"Oh, Tom, I reckon we're goners! And I reckon there ain't no mistake about where *I'll* go to, I been so wicked."

"Dad fetch it! I might 'a' been good, like Sid, if I'd 'a' tried—but no, I wouldn't, of course. But if I get off this time, I lay I'll just *waller* in Sunday schools!" And Tom began to snuffle.

"*You* bad!" and Huckleberry began to snuffle too. "Confound it, Tom Sawyer, you're just old pie, 'longside o' what *I* am!"

Tom choked off: "Look, Hucky! He's got his *back* to us!"

Hucky looked, with joy in his heart. "Well, he has, by jingoes! Did he before?"

"Yes, he did. But I never thought. Oh, this is bully, you know. *Now* who can he mean?"

The howling stopped. Tom pricked up his ears. "Sh! What's that?" he whispered.

"Sounds like—like hogs grunting. No—it's somebody snoring, Tom. I bleeve it's down at t'other end."

The spirit of adventure rose in the boys' souls once more.

"Hucky, do you dast to go if I lead?"

"I don't like to, much. Tom, s'pose it's Injun Joe!"

Tom quailed. But the temptation rose up strong again and the boys agreed to try, with the understanding that they would take to their heels if the snoring stopped. So they went tiptoeing stealthily down. When they had got to within five steps of the snorer, Tom stepped on a stick, and it broke with a snap. The man writhed a little, and his face came into the moonlight. It was Muff Potter.

The boys' hearts had stood still when the man moved, but their fears passed away now. They tiptoed out, through the broken weatherboarding, and stopped to exchange a parting word. That long howl rose on the night air again! They turned and saw the strange dog standing within a few feet of where Potter was lying, and *facing* Potter, with his nose pointing heavenward.

"Oh, geeminy, it's *him!*" exclaimed both boys, in a breath.

"Say, Tom—they say a stray dog come howling around Johnny Miller's house, 'bout midnight, two weeks ago; but there ain't anybody dead there yet."

"Well, I know that. And suppose there ain't. Didn't Gracie Miller fall in the kitchen fire and burn herself terrible the very next Saturday?"

"Yes, but she ain't *dead*. She's getting better."

"All right, you wait and see. She's a goner, just as sure as Muff Potter's a goner."

Then they separated. When Tom crept in at his bedroom window the night was almost spent. He fell asleep congratulating himself that nobody knew of his escapade. He was not aware that the gently snoring Sid was awake, and had been for an hour.

When Tom awoke, Sid was dressed and gone. There was a late look in the light, and he was startled. Why had he not been called—persecuted till he was up, as usual? The thought filled him with bodings. Within five minutes he was dressed and downstairs, feeling sore and drowsy. The family were still at table. There was no voice of rebuke; but there were averted eyes; there was a silence and an air of solemnity that struck a chill to the culprit's heart. He sat down and tried to seem gay, but it was uphill work; it roused no smile, no response.

After breakfast his aunt took him aside, and Tom almost brightened in the hope that he was going to be flogged; but it was not so. His aunt wept over him and asked him how he could break her old heart so; and finally told him to go on, and ruin himself, and bring her gray hairs with sorrow to the grave, for it was no use for her to try anymore. This was worse than a thousand whippings. Tom cried, he pleaded for forgiveness, and when he received his dismissal, was too miserable even to feel revengeful toward Sid.

He moped to school, gloomy and sad, and took his flogging for playing hookey the day before, with the air of one whose heart was busy with heavier woes and wholly dead to trifles. Then he betook himself to his seat, rested his elbows on his desk and his jaws in his hands, and stared at the wall with the stony stare of suffering. His elbow was pressing against some hard substance. After a long time he slowly and sadly changed his position, and took up this object. It was in a paper. He unrolled it. A long, lingering sigh followed, and his heart broke. It was his brass andiron knob!

This final feather broke the camel's back.

CHAPTER VII 7

CLOSE UPON NOON the whole village was suddenly electrified with the ghastly news. No need of the as yet undreamed-of telegraph; from house to house the tale flew with telegraphic speed. Of course the schoolmaster gave holiday for that afternoon; the town would have thought strangely of him if he had not.

A gory knife had been found close to the murdered man, and it had been recognized as belonging to Muff Potter—so the story ran—and a belated citizen had come upon Potter washing himself in the "branch"—suspicious circumstances—for washing was not a habit with Potter. It was said that the town had been ransacked for this "murderer" (the public are not slow in the matter of sifting evidence and arriving at a verdict) but that he could not be found. Horsemen had departed in every direction and the sheriff "was confident" that he would be captured before night.

All the town was drifting toward the graveyard. Tom's heartbreak vanished and he joined the procession, not because he would not a thousand times rather go anywhere else but because an awful, unaccountable fascination drew him. Arrived at the dreadful place, he wormed his small body through the crowd and saw the dismal spectacle. Somebody pinched his arm. He turned, and his eyes met

Huckleberry's. Then both looked elsewhere at once, and wondered if anybody had noticed anything in their glances. But everybody was intent upon the spectacle before them. "Poor young fellow!" "This ought to be a lesson to grave robbers!" "Muff Potter'll hang for this!" Such was the drift of remark; and the minister said, "It was a judgment; His hand is here."

Now Tom shivered from head to heel; for his eye fell upon the stolid face of Injun Joe. At this moment the crowd began to struggle, and voices shouted, "It's him! It's Muff Potter! He's coming!"

The crowd fell apart, now, and the sheriff came through, ostentatiously leading Potter by the arm. The poor fellow's face was haggard and fearful. When he stood before the murdered man, he shook as with a palsy and burst into tears. "I didn't do it," he sobbed; " 'pon my honor I never done it."

"Who's accused you?" shouted a voice.

This shot seemed to carry home. Potter lifted his face with pathetic hopelessness. He saw Injun Joe, and exclaimed, "Oh, Injun Joe, you promised me—"

"Is that your knife?" and it was thrust before him by the sheriff.

Potter would have fallen if they had not caught him. Then he said, "Something told me t' come back and get—" He shuddered, then said, "Tell 'em, Joe, tell 'em—it ain't any use anymore."

Then Huckleberry and Tom stood dumb and staring, and heard the stonyhearted liar reel off his serene statement of Potter's guilt, they expecting every moment that the clear sky would deliver God's lightnings upon his head. And when he had finished and still stood alive and whole, their wavering impulse to break their oath and save the poor betrayed prisoner's life vanished away, for plainly this miscreant had sold himself to Satan and it would be fatal to meddle with the property of such a power as that.

"Why didn't you leave? What did you want to come here for?" somebody said.

"I couldn't help it—" Potter moaned. "I couldn't seem to come anywhere but here." And he fell to sobbing again.

Injun Joe repeated his statement, just as calmly, a few minutes afterward at the inquest, under oath. He was now become, to the boys, the most balefully interesting object they had ever looked upon, and they could not take their fascinated eyes from his face. They inwardly resolved to watch him, nights, when opportunity should offer, in the hope of getting a glimpse of his dread master.

TOM'S FEARFUL SECRET disturbed his sleep for a week after this; and at breakfast one morning Sid said, "Tom, you talk in your sleep so much that you keep me awake."

Tom blanched and dropped his eyes.

"It's a bad sign," said Aunt Polly gravely. "What you got on your mind, Tom?"

"Nothing. Nothing 't I know of." But the boy's hand shook so that he spilled his coffee.

"And you do talk such stuff," Sid said. "Last night you said, 'It's blood, it's blood, that's what it is!' And you said, 'Don't torment me so—I'll tell!' Tell *what?*"

Everything was swimming before Tom. There is no telling what might have happened, now, but luckily Aunt Polly came to Tom's relief without knowing it. She said, "Sho! It's that dreadful murder. I dream about it 'most every night myself. Sometimes I dream it's me that done it."

Mary said she had been affected much the same way. Sid seemed satisfied. After that Tom complained of toothache for a week, and tied up his jaws every night. His distress of mind wore off gradually and the toothache grew irksome and was discarded.

Every day or two, Tom watched his opportunity and went to the little grated jail window and smuggled such small comforts through to the "murderer" as he could get hold of. The jail was a trifling little brick den that stood in a marsh at the edge of the village, and no guards were afforded for it; indeed it was seldom occupied. These offerings greatly helped to ease Tom's conscience.

The villagers had a strong desire to tar and feather Injun Joe and ride him on a rail for body snatching, but nobody was willing to take the lead in the matter, so it was dropped. He had been careful to begin both of his inquest statements with the fight, without confessing the grave robbery that preceded it; therefore it was deemed wisest not to try the case in the courts at present.

Then Tom's mind found a new and weighty interest. Becky Thatcher had stopped coming to school. She was ill. What if she should die! Tom began to hang around her father's house, nights, and feel miserable. He no longer took an interest in war, and he put his hoop away, and his bat; there was no joy in them anymore.

His aunt was concerned. She began to try all manner of remedies on him. She was one of those people who are infatuated with patent medicines and all newfangled methods of producing health or mending it. The water treatment was new, now, and Tom's low condition was a windfall to her. She had him out at daylight every morning, stood him up in the woodshed and deluged him with cold water; then she scrubbed him down with a towel like a file; then she rolled him up in a wet sheet and put him away under blankets till she sweated his soul clean. Notwithstanding all this, the boy grew more and more melancholy and pale. She added hot baths, sitz baths and shower baths. The boy remained as dismal as a hearse. She began to assist the water with a slim oatmeal diet and blister plasters, and calculating his capacity as she would a jug's, she filled him up every day with quack cure-alls.

Tom had become indifferent to persecution by this time. This filled the old lady with consternation. This indifference must be broken up at any cost. Now she heard of Pain-killer for the first time. She ordered a lot, tasted it and was filled with gratitude. It was simply fire in a liquid form. She gave Tom a teaspoonful and watched anxiously for the result. Her soul was instantly at peace; for the boy could not have shown a wilder, heartier interest if she had built a fire under him.

Tom had felt that it was time to wake up; this sort of life might be romantic, but it was getting to have too much distracting variety. So he had thought over various plans for relief, and had hit upon that of professing to be fond of Pain-killer. He asked for it so often that his aunt ended by telling him to help himself and quit bothering her. She watched the bottle clandestinely, and found that the medicine did really diminish. But it did not occur to her that the boy was mending the health of a crack in the floor with it.

One day Tom was dosing the crack when his aunt's yellow cat came along, purring, eyeing the teaspoon avariciously and begging for a taste. Tom said, "Don't ask for it unless you want it, Peter."

But Peter signified that he did want it.

"You better make sure."

Peter was sure.

"Now you've asked for it, and if you find you don't like it, you mustn't blame anybody but your own self."

Peter was agreeable. So Tom pried his mouth open and poured down the Pain-killer. Peter sprang a couple of yards in the air, and then delivered a war whoop and set off round the room, banging against furniture and upsetting flowerpots. Next he rose on his hind feet and pranced around, in a frenzy of enjoyment, his voice proclaiming happiness. Aunt Polly entered in time to see him throw a few double somersets, deliver a final mighty hurrah and sail through the open window, carrying the rest of the flowerpots with him. The old lady stood petrified with astonishment, peering over her glasses; Tom lay on the floor expiring with laughter.

"Tom, what on earth ails that cat?"

"*I* don't know, Aunt," gasped the boy.

"Why, I never see anything like it. What *did* make him act so?"

"'Deed I don't know, Aunt Polly; cats always act so when they're having a good time."

"They do, do they?" The old lady bent down. The handle of the telltale teaspoon was visible under the bed valance. Aunt Polly held it up. Tom winced and dropped his eyes. Aunt Polly cracked his head soundly with her thimble.

"Now, sir, why did you want to treat that poor dumb beast so?"

"I done it out of pity for him—because he hadn't any aunt."

"Hadn't any aunt! What has that got to do with it?"

"Heaps. Because if he'd 'a' had one she'd 'a' burned him out herself! She'd 'a' roasted his bowel out of him 'thout any more feeling than if he was a human!"

Aunt Polly felt a sudden pang of remorse. This was putting the thing in a new light; what was cruelty to a cat *might* be cruelty to a boy, too. She put her hand on Tom's head and said gently,

"I was meaning for the best, Tom. And, Tom, it *did* do you good."

Tom looked up in her face with just a perceptible twinkle peeping through his gravity. "I know you was meaning for the best, Auntie, and so was I with Peter. It done *him* good, too. I never see him get around so since—"

"Oh, go 'long with you, Tom. You try and be a good boy, for once, and you needn't take any more medicine."

Tom reached school ahead of time, a strange thing that had been occurring every day latterly. And now, as usual of late, he hung about the gate of the school yard instead of playing with his comrades. He was sick, he said, and he looked it. He tried to seem to be looking everywhere but whither he really was looking—down the road—hoping whenever a frisking frock came in sight, and hating the owner of it as soon as he saw she was not the right one.

At last frocks ceased to appear, and he dropped hopelessly into the "dumps." Then one more frock passed in at the gate, and Tom's heart gave a great bound. The next instant he was "going on" like an Indian; yelling, laughing, chasing boys, throwing handsprings, doing all the heroic things he could conceive of. But Becky Thatcher seemed to be unconscious of it all; she never looked. Was it possible that she was not aware that he was there? He carried his exploits to her immediate vicinity; war-whooped, snatched a boy's cap, hurled it away, broke through a group of boys and fell sprawling under Becky's nose, almost upsetting her—and she turned, with her nose in the air, and he heard her say: "Mf! Some people think they're mighty smart—always showing off!"

Tom's cheeks burned. He gathered himself up and sneaked off, crushed and crestfallen.

CHAPTER VIII 8

TOM'S MIND WAS MADE UP. He was a forsaken, friendless boy; nobody loved him; when they found out what they had driven him to, perhaps they would be sorry; he had tried to do right and get along, but they would not let him. Yes, they had forced him to it at last: he would run away, become a pirate and lead a life of crime.

By this time he was far down Meadow Lane, and the bell for school to "take up" tinkled faintly upon his ear. He sobbed, now, to think he should never, never hear that old familiar sound anymore; since he was driven out into the cold world, he must submit—but he forgave them. Then the sobs came thick and fast.

Just at this point he met his soul's sworn comrade, Joe Harper. Tom, wiping his eyes with his sleeve, began to blubber out something about a resolution to escape from hard usage and lack of sympathy at home by roaming abroad into the great world; and ended by hoping that Joe would not forget him.

But it transpired that this was a request which Joe had just been going to make of Tom, and had come to hunt him up for that purpose. His mother had whipped him for drinking some cream which he had never tasted and knew nothing about; it was plain that she was tired of him and wished him to go; if she felt that way, there was nothing for him to do but succumb; he hoped she would be happy, and never regret having driven her poor boy out into the unfeeling world to suffer or die.

As the two boys walked sorrowing along, they made a new compact to stand by each other till death relieved them of their troubles. Then they began to lay plans. Joe was for being a hermit, and living on crusts in a remote cave; but after listening to Tom, he conceded that there might be some advantages about a life of crime, and so he consented to be a pirate.

Below St. Petersburg, where the Mississippi was a trifle over a mile wide, there was a long, narrow, wooded island, with a shallow bar at the head of it. It was not inhabited; it lay close to the further shore, abreast a dense forest. So Jackson's Island was chosen. Who were to be the subjects of their piracies was a matter that did not occur to them. Then they hunted up Huckleberry Finn, and he joined them promptly, for all careers were one to him.

They presently separated, to meet at a spot on the riverbank two miles above the village at the favorite hour—midnight. There was a small log raft there which they meant to capture. Each would bring hooks and lines, and such provision as he could steal in the most dark and mysterious way—as became outlaws. Before the afternoon was done, they had all managed to enjoy the sweet glory of spreading the fact that pretty soon the town would "hear something." All who got this vague hint were cautioned to "be mum and wait."

About midnight Tom arrived with a boiled ham and a few trifles, and stopped in a dense undergrowth on a small bluff overlooking the meeting place. It was starlight, and very still. The mighty river lay like an ocean at rest. Tom listened a moment. Then he gave a low, distinct whistle. It was answered from under the bluff, and a guarded voice said, "Who goes there?"

"Tom Sawyer, the Black Avenger of the Spanish Main. Name your names."

"Huck Finn the Red-Handed, and Joe Harper the Terror of the Seas." Tom had furnished these titles from his favorite literature.

" 'Tis well. Give the countersign."

Two hoarse whispers delivered the same awful word simultaneously to the brooding night: "BLOOD!"

Then Tom let himself down over the bluff, tearing skin and clothes to some extent in the effort. There was an easy, comfortable path along the shore under the bluff, but it lacked the advantages of difficulty and danger so valued by a pirate.

The Terror of the Seas had brought a side of bacon, and had about worn himself out with getting it there. Finn the Red-Handed had stolen a skillet and a quantity of half-cured leaf tobacco, and had brought a few corncobs to make pipes with, though none of the pirates smoked but himself. The Black Avenger of the Spanish Main said it would never do to start without some fire. That was a wise thought; matches were hardly known there in that day. They saw a fire smoldering upon a great raft a hundred yards above, and they went stealthily thither and helped themselves to a chunk. They made an imposing adventure of it, saying, "Hist!" every now and then, and halting with finger on lip, hands on imaginary dagger hilts; and giving whispered orders that if "the foe" stirred, to "let him have it to the hilt." They knew the raftsmen were all at the village laying in stores or having a spree, but that was no excuse for conducting this thing in an unpiratical way.

They shoved off, presently, Tom in command, Huck at the after oar and Joe forward. Tom stood gloomy-browed, with folded arms, and gave his orders. "Luff, and bring her to the wind!"

"Aye, aye, sir!"

"Steady, steady-y-y-y!"

"Steady it is, sir!"

As the boys were monotonously driving the raft toward midstream it was understood that these orders were given only for "style," and were not intended to mean anything in particular.

"What sail's she carrying?"

"Courses, tops'ls and flying jib, sir."

"Send the r'yals up! Lively, now!"

"Aye, aye, sir!"

When the raft drew beyond the middle of the river, the boys pointed her head right, and then lay on their oars to travel with the current. Hardly a word was said during the next hour. Now the raft was passing the distant town. Two or three glimmering lights showed where it lay, peacefully sleeping, beyond the vague vast sweep of star-gemmed water. The Black Avenger stood still with folded arms, "looking his last" upon the scene of his former joys and his later sufferings, and wishing "she" could see him now, abroad on the wild sea, facing peril and death with a grim smile on his lips. It was but a small strain on his imagination to remove Jackson's Island beyond eyeshot of the village, and so he "looked his last" with a broken and satisfied heart.

About two o'clock in the morning the raft grounded on the bar above the head of the island, and they waded back and forth until they had landed their freight. Part of the raft's belongings consisted of an old sail, and this they spread over a nook in the bushes for a tent to shelter their provisions; but they themselves would sleep in the open air, as became outlaws.

They built a fire against the side of a great log in the forest, and then cooked some bacon in the frying pan for supper, and used up half of the corn-pone stock they had brought. It seemed glorious sport to be feasting in that wild free way in the virgin forest of an unexplored island, while the climbing fire lit up their faces, and they said they never would return to civilization. When the last crisp slice of bacon was gone, they stretched themselves out on the grass, filled with contentment. "*Ain't* it gay?" said Joe.

"It's *nuts!*" said Tom. "What would the boys say if they could see us?"

"Say? Well, they'd just die to be here—hey, Hucky!"

"I reckon so," said Huckleberry; "anyways, *I'm* suited. I don't want nothing better. I don't ever get enough to eat, gen'ally—and here they can't come and pick at a feller."

"It's just the life for me," said Tom. "You don't have to get up, mornings, and you don't have to go to school, and wash, and all that foolishness. You see a pirate don't have to do *anything*, Joe, when he's ashore, but a hermit *he* has to be praying considerable."

"Yes, that's so," said Joe, "but I hadn't thought much about it, you know. I'd a good deal rather be a pirate, now that I've tried it."

"And then," said Tom, "a hermit's got to sleep on the hardest place he can find, and put sackcloth and ashes on his head, and—"

"What does he put sackcloth and ashes on his head for?" inquired Huck.

"*I* dono. But they've *got* to. You'd have to if you was a hermit."

"Dern'd if I would," said Huck. "I'd run away." He had now finished gouging out a cob, and when he had fitted a weed stem to it, he loaded it with tobacco and pressed a coal to it. As he blew out a cloud of fragrant smoke the other pirates envied him this majestic vice, and secretly resolved to acquire it shortly. Presently Huck said, "What does pirates have to do?"

Tom said, "Oh, they have a bully time—take ships and burn them, and get the money and bury it, and kill everybody in the ships—make 'em walk a plank."

"And they carry the women to their island," said Joe; "they don't kill the women."

"No," assented Tom, "they don't kill the women—they're too noble. And the women's always beautiful, too."

"And they wear the bulliest clothes! All gold and silver and di'monds," said Joe.

"Who?" said Huck.

"Why, the pirates."

Gradually drowsiness began to steal upon them. The pipe dropped from the fingers of the Red-Handed, and he slept the sleep of the conscience-free and the weary. The Terror of the Seas and the Black Avenger of the Spanish Main had more difficulty in getting to sleep. They said their prayers inwardly, and lying down, since there was nobody there to make them kneel and recite aloud; in truth, they had a mind not to say them, but they were afraid lest they call down a special thunderbolt from heaven. Then they hovered upon the verge of sleep—but an intruder came, now, that would not "down." It was conscience. They thought of the stolen meat, and tried to argue it away by reminding conscience that they had purloined sweetmeats and apples scores of times; but conscience was not to be appeased by such thin plausibilities; it seemed to them, in the end, that there was no getting around the stubborn fact that taking sweetmeats was only "hooking," while taking bacon and hams and such valuables was plain *stealing*—and there was a command against that in the Bible. So they inwardly resolved that their piracies should not again be sullied with the crime of stealing. Then conscience granted a truce, and these curiously inconsistent pirates fell peacefully to sleep.

WHEN TOM AWOKE in the morning, he wondered where he was. He sat up and rubbed his eyes and looked around. Then he comprehended. It was the cool gray dawn, and there was a delicious sense of repose in the deep pervading silence of the woods. Not a leaf stirred; beaded dewdrops stood upon the leaves and grasses. A white layer of ashes covered the fire, and a thin blue breath of smoke rose straight into the air. Joe and Huck still slept.

Now, far away in the woods a bird called; another answered; presently the hammering of a woodpecker was heard. Gradually the cool dim gray of the morning whitened, and as gradually sounds multiplied and life manifested itself. The marvel of nature shaking off sleep unfolded itself to the musing boy. A little green worm came crawling over a dewy leaf, lifting two thirds of his body into the air from time to time and "sniffing around," then proceeding again—for he was measuring, Tom said. Now a procession of ants appeared, from nowhere in particular; and now a brown-spotted ladybug climbed the dizzy height of a grass-blade, and Tom bent down close to it and said, "Ladybug, ladybug, fly away home, your house is on fire, your children's alone," and she took wing and went off to see about it—which did not surprise the boy, for he knew of old that this insect was credulous about conflagrations.

When long lances of sunlight began to pierce through the foliage, Tom stirred up the other pirates, and in a minute or two they all were stripped and tumbling over each other in the shallow limpid water of the white sandbar. A vagrant current in the river had carried off their raft, but this only gratified them, since its going was something like burning the bridge between them and civilization.

They came back to camp wonderfully refreshed and ravenous; and they soon had the campfire blazing up again. Huck found a spring of clear water close by, and the boys made cups of hickory leaves, and felt that water, sweetened with such a wildwood charm as that, would be a good-enough substitute for coffee. While Joe was slicing bacon for breakfast, Tom and Huck stepped to a nook in the riverbank and threw in their lines. Joe had not had time to get impatient before they were back again with some handsome bass, a couple of sun perch and a small catfish. They fried the fish with the bacon, and no fish had ever seemed so delicious before.

After breakfast they went off through the woods on an exploring expedition. They tramped gaily along, over decaying logs, through underbrush, among solemn monarchs of the forest hung with a drooping regalia of grapevines. Now and then they came upon snug nooks carpeted with grass and jeweled with flowers.

They found plenty of things to be delighted with, but nothing to be astonished at. They discovered that the island was about three miles long and a quarter mile wide, and that it was only separated from the eastern shore by a narrow channel hardly two hundred yards wide. They took a swim about every hour, so it was the middle of the afternoon when they got back to camp. Then they fared sumptuously upon cold ham, and threw themselves down in the shade to talk. But the talk soon began to drag. The solemnity that brooded in the woods, and the sense of loneliness, began to tell upon their spirits. They fell to thinking. A sort of undefined longing crept upon them. This took dim shape, presently—it was budding homesickness. Even Finn the Red-Handed was dreaming of his doorsteps and empty hogsheads. But they were all ashamed of their weakness, and none spoke his thought.

For some time, now, the boys had been dully conscious of a peculiar sound in the distance, just as one sometimes is of the ticking of a clock which he takes no distinct note of. But now this sound became pronounced, and forced a recognition. The boys started, glanced at each other, and then assumed a listening attitude. There was a long silence; then a deep, sullen boom.

"What is it!" exclaimed Joe, under his breath.

"I wonder," said Tom in a whisper. They waited a time that seemed an age, listening, and then the same muffled boom troubled the solemn hush. "Let's go and see."

They hurried to the shore toward the town, parted the bushes on the bank and peered out over the water. The little steam ferryboat was about a mile below the village, drifting with the current. Her deck seemed crowded with people. There were also a great many skiffs rowing about or floating with the stream. Presently a great jet of white smoke burst from the ferryboat's side, and as it expanded and rose in a lazy cloud, that same dull throb of sound was borne to the listeners again.

"I know now!" exclaimed Tom. "Somebody's drownded!"

"That's it," said Huck; "they done that when Bill Turner got drownded; they shoot a cannon over the water, and that makes him come up to the top."

"By jings, I wish I was over there, now," said Joe.

"I do too," said Huck. "I'd give heaps to know who it is."

The boys still listened and watched. Presently a revealing thought flashed through Tom's mind, and he exclaimed:

"Boys, I know who's drownded—it's us!"

They felt like heroes in an instant. Here was a gorgeous triumph; they were missed; they were mourned; tears were being shed; and best of all, the departed were the talk of the town, and the envy of all the boys, as far as this dazzling notoriety was concerned. This was fine. It was worthwhile to be a pirate, after all.

As twilight drew on, the ferryboat and the skiffs disappeared. The pirates returned to camp. Jubilant over their new grandeur, they caught fish, cooked supper and ate it, and then fell to guessing at what the village was saying about them. But when the shadows of night closed them in, they gradually ceased to talk, and sat gazing into the fire, with their minds evidently wandering elsewhere. The excitement was gone, now, and Tom and Joe could not keep back thoughts of certain persons at home who were not enjoying this fine frolic as much as they were. Misgivings came; and a sigh or two escaped unawares.

By and by, as the night deepened, Huck began to nod, and presently to snore. Joe followed next. Tom lay upon his elbow motionless for some time, watching the two. At last he got up cautiously, on his knees, and went searching in the grass. He picked up and inspected several semicylinders of the thin white bark of a sycamore, and finally chose two. Then he knelt by the fire and painfully wrote something upon each of these with his "red keel"; one he rolled up and put in his jacket pocket, and the other he put in Joe's hat. And he also put into the hat certain schoolboy treasures of almost inestimable value—a lump of chalk, an India-rubber ball and three fishhooks. Then he tiptoed his way among the trees till he felt that he was out of hearing, and straightway broke into a run in the direction of the sandbar.

A FEW MINUTES LATER Tom was in the shoal water of the bar, wading toward the Illinois shore. Before the depth reached his middle he was halfway over; and he struck out confidently to swim the remaining hundred yards. He swam quartering upstream, reached the shore finally and drew himself out. He put his hand on his jacket pocket, found his piece of bark safe, and then struck through the woods, following the shore. Shortly before ten o'clock he came out into an open place opposite the village, and saw the ferryboat lying in the shadow of the high bank. Everything was quiet under the stars. He crept down the bank, watching with all his eyes, slipped into the water, and climbed into the skiff that was tied to the ferryboat's stern. He laid himself down under the thwarts and waited, panting.

Presently the bell tapped and a voice gave the order to "cast off." A minute later the skiff's head was standing high up against the boat's swell, and the voyage was begun. Tom felt happy in his success, for he knew it was the boat's last trip for the night. At the end of fifteen minutes the wheels stopped, and Tom slipped overboard and swam ashore, landing fifty yards downstream, out of danger of possible stragglers.

He flew along unfrequented alleys, and shortly found himself at his aunt's back fence. He climbed over, and approached the sitting-room window, where a light was burning. There sat Aunt Polly, Sid, Mary, and Joe Harper's mother, talking. They were by the bed, and the bed was between them and the door. Tom went to the door and began to softly lift the latch; then he pressed gently, and the door yielded a crack; he continued pushing, quaking every time it creaked, till he judged he might squeeze through on his knees; so he put his head through and began, warily.

"What makes the candle blow so?" asked Aunt Polly. "Why that door's open, I believe. Go 'long and shut it, Sid."

Tom disappeared under the bed just in time. He lay and "breathed" himself for a time, and then crept to where he could almost touch his aunt's foot.

"But as I was saying," said Aunt Polly, "he warn't *bad*, so to say—only misch*ee*vous. He warn't any more responsible than a colt. *He* never meant any harm, and he was the best-hearted boy that ever was"—and she began to cry.

"It was just so with my Joe—always up to every kind of mischief, but he was just as unselfish and kind as he could be—and laws bless me, to think I went and whipped him for taking that cream, never once recollecting that I throwed it out myself because it was sour, and I never to see him again in this world, never, never, never, poor abused boy!" And Mrs. Harper sobbed as if her heart would break.

"I hope Tom's better off where he is," said Sid, "but if he'd been better in some ways—"

"*Sid!*" said Aunt Polly. "Not a word against my Tom, now that he's gone! God'll take care of *him*—never you trouble *yourself*, sir! Oh, Mrs. Harper, I don't know how to give him up! He was such a comfort to me, although he tormented my old heart out of me, 'most."

At this the old lady broke entirely down. Tom was snuffling now, himself, more in pity of himself than anybody else. He began to have a nobler opinion of himself than ever before. Still, he was sufficiently touched by his aunt's grief to long to rush out from under the bed and overwhelm her with joy—but he resisted.

He went on listening, and gathered by odds and ends that it was conjectured at first that the boys had got drowned while taking a swim; then the small raft had been missed; next, certain boys said the missing lads had promised that the village should "hear something" soon; the wiseheads had "put this and that together" and decided that the lads had gone off on that raft and would turn up at the next town below; but toward noon the raft had been found, lodged against the Missouri shore some five miles below the village—and then hope perished; they must be drowned, else hunger would have driven them home. It was believed that the drowning must have occurred in mid-channel, since the boys, being good swimmers, would otherwise have escaped to shore. This was Wednesday night. If the bodies continued missing until Sunday, all hope would be given over, and the funerals would be preached on that morning. Tom shuddered.

Mrs. Harper gave a sobbing good-night and rose to go. The two women flung themselves into each other's arms and had a good, consoling cry, and then parted. Aunt Polly was tender far beyond her wont, in her good-night to Sid and Mary. Sid snuffled a bit and Mary went off, crying with all her heart.

Aunt Polly knelt down and prayed for Tom so touchingly, so appealingly, and with such measureless love in her words and her old trembling voice, that he was soon weltering in tears again.

He had to keep still long after she went to bed, for she kept tossing unrestfully. But at last she was quiet, only moaning a little in her sleep. Now the boy stole out, rose gradually by the bedside, shaded the candlelight with his hand and stood regarding her. His heart was full of pity for her. He took out his sycamore scroll and placed it by the candle. But something occurred to him, and he lingered, considering. His face lighted with a happy solution of his thought; he put the bark hastily in his pocket. Then he bent over and kissed the faded lips, and straightway made his stealthy exit.

He threaded his way back to the ferry landing and walked boldly on board the boat, for he knew she was tenantless except for a watchman who always turned in and slept. He untied the skiff at the stern, slipped into it, and was soon rowing cautiously upstream. When he had pulled a mile above the village, he started across. He hit the landing on the other side neatly, for this was a familiar bit of work to him. Then he stepped ashore and entered the wood.

It was broad daylight before he found himself fairly abreast the island bar. He plunged into the stream. A little later he paused, dripping, upon the threshold of the camp, and heard Joe say:

"No, Tom's true-blue, Huck. He won't desert. He's up to something. Now I wonder what?"

"Well, the things is ours, anyway, ain't they?"

"Pretty near, but not yet. The writing says they are if he ain't back here to breakfast."

"Which he is!" exclaimed Tom, with fine dramatic effect, stepping grandly into camp.

A sumptuous breakfast of bacon and fish was shortly provided, and as the boys set to work upon it, Tom recounted (and adorned) his adventures. They were a vain and boastful company of heroes when the tale was done. Then Tom hid himself away in a shady nook to sleep, and the other pirates got ready to fish and explore.

CHAPTER IX

AFTER DINNER ALL THE GANG turned out to hunt for turtle eggs on the bar. They poked sticks into the sand, and when they found a soft place they dug with their hands. The eggs were round white things a trifle smaller than an English walnut. They had a famous fried-egg feast that night, and another on Friday morning.

After breakfast they went whooping and prancing out on the bar, and chased each other round and round, shedding clothes as they went, until they were naked, and then continued the frolic far away up the shoal water, against the stiff current, which latter tripped their legs from under them from time to time and greatly increased the fun. And now and then they stooped and splashed water in each other's faces, finally gripping and struggling till the best man ducked his neighbor, and then they all went under in a tangle of white legs and arms, and came up sputtering, laughing, and gasping for breath. When they were well exhausted, they would run out and sprawl on the dry, hot sand, and by and by break for the water again and go through the performance once more.

Finally they drew a ring in the sand and had a circus—with three clowns in it. Next they got their marbles and played knucks and ringtaw and keeps till that amusement grew stale. But by this time they all were tired. They gradually wandered apart, dropped into the "dumps," and fell to gazing across the river to where the village lay drowsing in the sun. Tom found himself writing *Becky* in the sand with his big toe. He scratched it out, and was angry with himself for his weakness. But he wrote it again, nevertheless; he could not help it. He erased it once more and then took himself out of temptation by driving the other boys together and joining them.

But Joe's spirits had gone down almost beyond resurrection. He was so homesick that he could hardly endure the misery of it. Huck was melancholy, too. Tom was downhearted, but tried not to show it. He had a secret which he was not ready to tell, yet, but if this mutinous depression was not broken up soon, he would have to bring it out. He said, with a great show of cheerfulness:

"I bet there's been pirates on this island before, boys. We'll explore it again. They've hid treasures here somewhere. How'd you feel to light on a rotten chest full of gold—hey?"

But it roused only a faint enthusiasm, which faded out, with no reply. Joe sat poking up the sand with a stick and looking very gloomy. Finally he said, "Oh, boys, let's give it up. I want to go home. It's lonesome."

"Joe, you'll feel better by and by," said Tom. "Just think of the fishing that's here."

"I don't care for fishing. I want to go home."

"But, Joe, there ain't such another swimming place anywhere."

"Swimming's no good. I don't seem to care for it, somehow, when there ain't anybody to say I shan't go in."

"Oh, shucks! Baby! You want to see your mother, I reckon."

"Yes, I *do* want to see my mother—and you would, too, if you had one." And Joe snuffled a little.

"Well, we'll let the crybaby go home to his mother, *won't* we Huck? *You* like it here, *don't* you, Huck?"

Huck said, "Y-e-s"—without any heart in it.

"I'll never speak to you again as long as I live," said Joe, rising. "There now!" And he moved moodily away and began to dress.

"Who cares!" said Tom. But he was uneasy, nevertheless, and alarmed to see Huck eyeing Joe's preparations so wistfully, and keeping up such an ominous silence. Presently, without a parting word, Joe began to wade off toward the Illinois shore. Tom's heart sank. He glanced at Huck, but Huck dropped his eyes. Then he said:

"I want to go, too, Tom. It was getting so lonesome, and now it'll be worse. Let's us go, too, Tom."

"I won't! You can all go, if you want to. I mean to stay."

"Tom, I better go."

"Well, go 'long—who's hendering you?"

Huck began to pick up his clothes. He said, "Tom, I wisht you'd come, too. We'll wait for you when we get to shore."

"Well, you'll wait a blame long time, that's all."

Huck started sorrowfully away, and Tom stood looking after him, with a strong desire tugging at him to yield his pride and go along too. He hoped the boys would stop, but they waded on. It suddenly dawned on Tom that it was very lonely and still. He made one final struggle with his pride, and then darted after his comrades, yelling, "Wait! Wait! I want to tell you something!"

They stopped and turned. When he got to where they were, he unfolded his secret, and when they saw the point he was driving at, they set up a war whoop, and said it was "splendid!" and said if he had told them at first, they wouldn't have started away. He made a plausible excuse; but his real reason had been the fear that not even the secret would keep them with him for long, and so he had held it in reserve as a last seduction.

The lads came gaily back, chattering about Tom's stupendous plan. After a dainty egg-and-fish dinner, Tom said he wanted to learn to smoke, now. Joe caught at the idea and said he would like to try, too. So Huck made pipes and filled them. These novices had never smoked anything before but cigars made of grapevine, and they "bit" the tongue, and were not considered manly anyway.

Now they stretched themselves out on their elbows and began to puff charily. The smoke had an unpleasant taste, and they gagged a little, but Tom said, "Why, it's just as easy! If I'd 'a' knowed *this* was all, I'd 'a' learnt long ago."

"So would I," said Joe. "It's just nothing."

"Why, many a time I've looked at people smoking, and thought well I wish I could do that; but I never thought I could," said Tom.

"That's just the way with me. I bleeve I could smoke this pipe all day," said Joe. "*I* don't feel sick."

"Neither do I," said Tom. "*I* could smoke it all day. But I bet you Jeff Thatcher couldn't."

"Jeff Thatcher! Why, he'd keel over just with two draws."

"I bet he would, Joe. Say—I wish the boys could see us now."

"So do I."

"Say—boys, don't say anything about it, and sometime when they're around, I'll come up to you and say, 'Joe, got a pipe? I want a smoke.' And then you'll out with the pipes, and we'll light up just as ca'm, and then just see 'em look!"

"By jings, that'll be gay, Tom!"

So the talk ran on. But presently it began to flag a trifle. The silences widened; the expectoration marvelously increased. Both boys were looking very pale and miserable, now. Joe's pipe dropped from his fingers. Tom's followed. Joe said feebly, "I've lost my knife. I reckon I better go and find it."

Tom said, with quivering lips, "I'll help you. You go that way and I'll hunt around by the spring. No, you needn't come, Huck—we can find it."

Huck waited an hour. Then he went to find his comrades. They were wide apart in the woods, both very pale, both fast asleep. But something informed him that if they had had any trouble they had got rid of it.

They were not talkative at supper that night. They had a humble look, and when Huck prepared his pipe after the meal and was going to prepare theirs, they said no, they were not feeling very well—something they ate at dinner had disagreed with them.

About midnight Joe awoke, and called the boys. There was a brooding oppressiveness in the air that seemed to bode something. The boys huddled together near the fire, though the dull dead heat of the atmosphere was stifling. Beyond the light of the fire everything was swallowed up in darkness. Presently there came a quivering glow that vaguely revealed the foliage for a moment and then vanished. By and by another came, a little stronger. Then another. Then a faint moan came sighing through the branches of the forest and the boys felt a fleeting breath upon their cheeks, and shuddered with the fancy that the Spirit of the Night had gone by. Now a weird flash turned night into day and showed every little grass-blade, separate and distinct, that grew about their feet. And it showed three white, startled faces, too. An instant crash followed that seemed to rend the treetops right over the boys' heads. A few big raindrops fell pattering upon the leaves.

"Quick, boys! Go for the tent!" exclaimed Tom.

They sprang away, stumbling over roots in the dark. A furious blast roared through the trees, making everything sing as it went. One blinding flash after another came, and peal on peal of deafening thunder. And now a drenching rain poured down and the rising hurricane drove it in sheets along the ground. One by one the boys straggled under the tent, cold, scared, and streaming with water. The old sail flapped furiously, the tempest rose higher and higher, and presently the sail tore loose from its fastenings and went winging away. The boys seized each other's hands and fled, to the shelter of a great oak that stood upon the riverbank.

Under the ceaseless conflagration of lightning that flamed in the skies, everything below stood out in shadowless distinctness: the bending trees, the river white with foam. Every little while some giant tree fell crashing; and the unflagging thunderpeals came now in earsplitting bursts, unspeakably appalling.

The storm culminated in one matchless effort that seemed likely to tear the island to pieces, drown it to the treetops, blow it away, and deafen every creature in it. But at last it retired, and its threatenings and grumblings grew weaker and weaker. The boys went back to camp, a good deal awed; but they found there was still something to be thankful for, because the great sycamore, the shelter of their beds, was a ruin now, blasted by the lightnings, and they were not under it when the catastrophe happened.

Everything in camp was drenched, the fire as well; for they had made no provision against rain. Here was a matter for dismay, for they were soaked through and chilled. But they presently discovered that the fire had eaten so far up under the great log it had been built against, that a handbreadth of it had escaped wetting; so they patiently wrought until, with shreds and bark gathered from the undersides of logs, they coaxed the fire to burn again. Then they piled on boughs till they had a roaring furnace, and were gladhearted once more. They dried their ham and had a feast, and after that they sat by the fire and glorified their midnight adventure until morning, for there was not a dry spot to sleep on.

As the sun began to steal in upon the boys, drowsiness came over them and they went out on the sandbar and lay down to sleep. They got scorched out by and by, and drearily set about getting breakfast. After the meal they felt rusty, and stiff-jointed, and a little homesick once more. Tom saw the signs, and fell to getting them interested in a new device. This was to knock off being pirates, for a while, and be Indians. They were attracted by this idea; so it was not long before they were stripped, and striped from head to heel with black mud, like so many zebras—all of them chiefs, of course—and then they separated into three hostile tribes, and killed and scalped each other by thousands. It was a gory day. Consequently it was an extremely satisfactory one.

When she found the entire fence not only whitewashed but elaborately coated and recoated, her astonishment was almost unspeakable.

All at once the doctor flung himself free, seized the heavy headboard of Williams' grave and felled Potter with it—and at the same time the half-breed saw his chance and drove the knife to the hilt in the young man's breast.

But as Tom stepped forward to go to his punishment the surprise, the gratitude, the adoration that shown upon him out of poor Becky's eyes seemed pay enough for a hundred floggings.

JF

They shoved off, presently, Tom in command, Huck at the after oar, and Joe forward.

When they reached the haunted house there was something so weird and grisly about the silence that reigned there under the baking sun that they were afraid, for a moment, to venture in.

"Can you find the way, Tom? It's all a mixed up crookedness to me."

MARK TWAIN

They assembled in camp toward suppertime, hungry and happy; but now a difficulty arose—hostile Indians could not break the bread of hospitality together without first making peace, and this was a simple impossibility without smoking a pipe of peace. Two of the savages almost wished they had remained pirates. However, there was no other way; so with such show of cheerfulness as they could muster they called for the pipe and took their whiff as it passed, in due form.

And behold, they were glad they had gone into savagery, for they had gained something; they found that they could now smoke a little without having to go and hunt for a lost knife. They practiced more after supper, with right fair success, and so spent a jubilant evening. We will leave them to smoke and chatter and brag, since we have no further use for them at present.

But there was no hilarity in the little town that same tranquil Saturday afternoon. The Harpers, and Aunt Polly's family, were being put into mourning, with great grief and many tears. The villagers conducted their concerns with an absent air, and talked little; but they sighed often. The Saturday holiday seemed a burden to the children. They had no heart in their sports, and gradually gave them up. Becky Thatcher moped about the deserted schoolhouse yard, but she found nothing there to comfort her. She soliloquized, "Oh, if I only had his brass andiron knob again! But I haven't got anything now to remember him by." She choked back a sob, and the tears rolled down her cheeks. "Oh, if it was to do over again, I wouldn't say that! But he's gone now; and I'll never never see him anymore!"

The next morning, when the Sunday-school hour was finished, the bell began to toll instead of ringing in the usual way. It was a very still Sabbath, and the mournful sound seemed in keeping with the musing hush that lay upon nature. The villagers began to gather, loitering a moment in the vestibule to converse in whispers. But there was no whispering in the church; only the funereal rustling of dresses as the women gathered to their seats. Then Aunt Polly entered, and Sid and Mary and the Harper family, all in deep black; and the whole congregation, the old minister as well, rose reverently and stood until the mourners were seated in the front pew. And then the minister spread his hands abroad and prayed. A moving hymn was sung, and the text followed: "*I am the resurrection and the life . . .*"

As the service proceeded, the clergyman drew such pictures of the graces, the winning ways and the rare promise of the lost lads, and related so many touching incidents from their lives, that every soul there, thinking he recognized these pictures, felt a pang that he had persistently blinded himself to them always before, and had as persistently seen only faults and flaws in the poor boys. The congregation became more and more moved as the pathetic tale went on, till at last the whole company broke down and joined the mourners in a chorus of anguished sobs, the preacher himself giving way to his feelings, and crying in the pulpit.

There was a rustle in the gallery; a moment later the church door creaked; the minister raised his streaming eyes above his handkerchief, and stood transfixed! First one and then another pair of eyes followed the minister's, and then almost with one impulse the congregation rose and stared while the three dead boys came marching up the aisle, Tom in the lead, Joe next, and Huck sneaking sheepishly in the rear! They had been hid in the gallery listening to their own funeral sermon!

Aunt Polly, Mary and the Harpers threw themselves upon their restored ones and smothered them with kisses, while poor Huck stood abashed and uncomfortable. He wavered, and started to slink away, but Tom seized him and said, "Aunt Polly, it ain't fair. Somebody's got to be glad to see Huck."

"And so they shall. *I'm* glad to see him, poor motherless thing!" And the loving attentions which Aunt Polly then lavished upon Huckleberry were the one thing capable of making him more uncomfortable than he had been before.

Suddenly the minister shouted at the top of his voice: "*Praise God from whom all blessings flow*—SING!" And they did. "Old Hundred" swelled up with a triumphant burst, and while it shook the rafters Tom Sawyer the Pirate looked around upon the envying juveniles about him and confessed in his heart that this was the proudest moment of his life.

Tom got more cuffs and kisses that day—according to Aunt Polly's varying moods—than he had earned before in a year; and he hardly knew which expressed the most gratefulness to God and affection for himself.

CHAPTER X

THAT HAD BEEN TOM'S great secret—the scheme to return home with his brother pirates and attend their own funerals. They had paddled over to the Missouri shore on a log, at dusk on Saturday, landing five or six miles below the village; they had slept in the woods at the edge of the town till nearly daylight, and had then crept through back lanes and finished their sleep in the unused gallery of the church among a chaos of invalided benches.

At breakfast, Monday, Aunt Polly and Mary were very loving and attentive to Tom. There was an unusual amount of talk. In the course of it Aunt Polly said, "Well, I don't say it wasn't a fine joke to keep everybody suffering 'most a week so you boys had a good time, but it is a pity you could let *me* suffer so. If you could come over on a log to go to your funeral, you could have come over and give me a hint someway that you warn't *dead*."

"Yes, you could have done that, Tom," said Mary; "and I believe you would if you had thought of it."

"Would you, Tom, if you'd thought of it?" said Aunt Polly, her face lighting wistfully.

"I—well, I don't know. 'Twould 'a' spoiled everything."

"Tom, I hoped you loved me that much," said Aunt Polly, with a grieved tone. "It would have been something if you'd cared enough to *think* of it, even if you didn't *do* it."

"I dreamed about you anyway, Auntie," said Tom, feeling repentant. "That's something, ain't it?"

"It's better than nothing. What did you dream?"

"Why, Wednesday night I dreamed that you was sitting over

there by the bed, and Sid was sitting by the woodbox, and Mary next to him. And Joe Harper's mother was here."

"Why, she *was* here! Did you dream any more?"

"Oh, lots. But it's so dim, now."

"Well, *try* to recollect—can't you?"

"Somehow it seems to me that the wind—the wind blowed the—the—" Tom pressed his fingers on his forehead and then said, "I've got it now! It blowed the candle! And you said, 'Why, I believe that that door—that door is open.'"

"As I'm sitting here, I did! Didn't I, Mary! Go on!"

"And then—and then—well I won't be certain, but it seems like as if you made Sid go and—and—shut it."

"Well, for the land's sake! I never heard the beat of that. Don't tell *me* there ain't anything in dreams. Go on, Tom!"

"Oh, it's all getting bright as day, now. Next you said I warn't *bad*, only misch*ee*vous, and not any more responsible than—than—I think it was a colt. And then you began to cry."

"So I did. Not the first time, neither. And then—"

"Then Mrs. Harper she began to cry, and said Joe was just the same, and she wished she hadn't whipped him for taking cream when she'd throwed it out her own self—"

"Tom! The sperrit was upon you! Land alive, go on, Tom!"

"And after a while there was a lot of talk 'bout dragging the river for us, and 'bout having the funeral, and then you and old Mrs. Harper hugged and cried, and she went."

"It happened just so!"

"Then I thought you prayed for me—and you went to bed, and I was so sorry, that I took and wrote on a piece of sycamore bark, 'We ain't dead, we are only off being pirates,' and put it on the table by the candle; and then you looked so good, laying there asleep, that I thought I leaned over and kissed you on the lips."

"Did you, Tom, *did* you! I just forgive you everything for that!" And she seized the boy in a crushing embrace that made him feel like the guiltiest of villains.

"It was very kind, even though it was only a—dream," Sid soliloquized just audibly.

"Shut up, Sid! A body does just the same in a dream as he'd do if he was awake. Here's the big apple I've been saving for you, Tom. Now go 'long to school. I'm thankful to the good God and Father of us all I've got you back. Go 'long, Sid, Mary, Tom—you've hendered me long enough."

The children left for school. What a hero Tom was become, now! He did not go skipping and prancing, but moved with a dignified swagger as became a pirate who felt that the public eye was on him. As indeed it was; he tried not to seem to see the looks or hear the remarks as he passed along, but they were food and drink to him. Smaller boys than himself flocked at his heels; and at school the children made so much of him and of Joe Harper that the two heroes were not long in becoming insufferably stuck-up. The very summit of glory was reached when they began to tell their adventures to hungry listeners—but they only began; it was not a thing likely to have an end, with imaginations like theirs to furnish material.

Tom decided now that he could be independent of Becky Thatcher. Now that he was distinguished, maybe she would be wanting to "make up." Well, let her—she should see that he could be as indifferent as some other people. Presently she arrived. Tom pretended not to see her. He moved away and joined a group of boys and girls and began to talk. Soon he observed that she was tripping gaily back and forth with flushed face and dancing eyes, pretending to be busy chasing schoolmates, and screaming with laughter when she made a capture; but he noticed that she always made her captures in his vicinity, and that she cast a conscious eye in his direction at such times, too. It gratified all the vicious vanity that was in him; and so, instead of winning him, it only "set him up" the more and made him the more diligent to avoid betraying that he knew she was about.

Presently she gave over skylarking, and moved irresolutely about, sighing once or twice and glancing furtively and wistfully toward Tom. Then she observed that now Tom was talking more particularly to Amy Lawrence than to anyone else. She felt a sharp pang and tried to go away, but her feet were treacherous, and carried her to the group instead. She said to a girl almost at Tom's elbow—with sham vivacity, "Why, Mary Austin! You bad girl, why didn't you come to Sunday school?"

"I did come—didn't you see me? I saw *you.*"

"Did you? Well, I wanted to tell you about the picnic. My ma's going to let me have one."

"Oh, goody; I hope she'll let *me* come."

"She will. The picnic's for me. She'll let anybody come that I want, and I want you."

"That's ever so nice. When is it going to be?"

"By and by. Maybe about vacation."

"You going to have all the girls and boys?"

"Yes, everyone that's friends to me—or wants to be," and she glanced at Tom, but he talked right along to Amy Lawrence about the terrible storm on the island, and how the lightning tore the great sycamore tree "all to flinders" while he was "standing within three feet of it."

"Oh, may I come?" said Gracie Miller.

"Yes."

"And me, too?" said Susy Harper. "And Joe?"

"Yes."

And so on, till all the group had begged for invitations but Tom and Amy. Then Tom turned coolly away, still talking, and took Amy with him. Becky's lips trembled and the tears came to her eyes; she hid these signs and went on chattering, but the life had gone out of the picnic, now; she got away as soon as she could and hid herself and had what her sex call a good cry. Then she sat moody, with wounded pride, till the bell rang. She roused up, now, and gave her plaited tails a shake and said she knew what *she'd* do.

At recess Tom continued his flirtation with Amy with jubilant self-satisfaction. And he kept drifting about to find Becky and lacerate her with the performance. At last he spied her, but there was a sudden falling of his mercury. She was sitting cozily on a little bench behind the schoolhouse looking at a picture book with Alfred Temple—and so absorbed were they, and their heads so close together over the book, that they did not seem to be conscious of anything in the world besides.

Jealousy ran red-hot through Tom's veins. He began to hate himself for throwing away the chance Becky had offered for a reconciliation. Amy chatted happily along, as they walked, but Tom's tongue had lost its function. Soon her happy prattle became intolerable. Tom hinted at things he had to attend to, and leaving her, he hastened away.

Any other boy! Tom thought, grating his teeth. Any boy but that St. Louis smarty! Oh, all right, I licked you the first day you ever saw this town, mister, and I'll lick you again. You just wait till I catch you out!

At noon Tom fled home; his jealousy could bear no more. Becky resumed her picture inspections with Alfred, but as the minutes dragged along and no Tom came to suffer, her triumph began to cloud and she lost interest. When poor Alfred, seeing that he was losing her, he did not know how, kept exclaiming, "Oh, here's a jolly one! Look at this!" she lost patience at last, and said, "Oh, don't bother me! I don't care for them!" and burst into tears, and got up and walked away.

Alfred went musing into the deserted schoolhouse. He was humiliated and angry. He easily guessed his way to the truth—the girl had simply made a convenience of him to vent her spite upon Tom Sawyer. He was far from hating Tom the less when this thought occurred to him. He wished there was some way to get that boy into trouble without much risk to himself. Tom's spelling book fell under his eye. Here was his opportunity. He gratefully opened to the lesson for the afternoon and poured ink upon the page.

Becky, glancing in at a window behind him at the moment, saw the act, and moved on. She started homeward, now, intending to find Tom and tell him; Tom would be thankful and their troubles would be healed. Before she was halfway home, however, she had changed her mind. The thought of Tom's treatment of her when she was talking about the picnic came scorching back and filled her with shame. She resolved to let him get whipped on the damaged spelling book's account, and to hate him forever, into the bargain.

Poor girl, she did not know how fast she was nearing trouble herself. The master, Mr. Dobbins, had reached middle age with an unsatisfied ambition. The darling of his desires was to be a doctor, but poverty had decreed that he should be nothing higher than a village schoolmaster. Every day he took a mysterious book out of his desk and absorbed himself in it when no classes were reciting. He kept that book under lock and key. Every boy and girl in school had a theory about the nature of that book; but no two theories were alike, and there was no way of getting at the facts in the case.

Now, as Becky returned to school and was passing by Mr. Dobbins' desk, which stood near the door, she noticed that the key was in the lock! It was a precious moment. She glanced around; found herself alone, and the next instant she had the book in her hands. The title page—Professor Somebody's *Anatomy*—carried no information to her mind; so she began to turn the leaves. She came at once upon a handsomely engraved and colored frontispiece—a human figure, stark naked. At that moment Tom Sawyer stepped in at the door and caught a glimpse of the picture. Becky snatched at the book to close it, and had the hard luck to tear the pictured plate half down the middle. She thrust the volume into the desk, turned the key, and burst out crying with vexation.

"Tom Sawyer, you are just as mean as you can be, to sneak up on a person and look at what they're looking at."

"How could *I* know you was looking at anything?"

"You ought to be ashamed, Tom Sawyer; you know you're going to tell on me, and oh, what shall I do! I'll be whipped, and I never was whipped in school." Then she stamped her little foot and said, "*Be* so mean if you want to! Hateful, hateful, hateful!" And she flung out of the house with a new explosion of crying.

Tom stood still, rather flustered by this onslaught. Presently he said to himself:

What a curious kind of a fool a girl is! Never been licked in school! Shucks. What's a licking! Well, of course *I* ain't going to tell old Dobbins on this little fool, because there's other ways of getting even on her that ain't so mean; but what of it? Old Dobbins will ask who it was tore his book. Nobody'll answer. Then he'll ask first one and then t'other, and when he comes to the right girl he'll know it. Girls' faces always tell. She'll get licked. Well, there ain't any way out of it for Becky Thatcher. Tom conned the thing a moment longer and then added: All right, though; she'd like to see me in just such a fix—let her sweat it out!

In a few moments the master arrived and school "took in." Tom did not feel a strong interest in his studies. Every time he stole a glance at the girls' side of the room Becky's face troubled him. Presently the spelling-book discovery was made, and Tom's mind was entirely full of his own matters for a while after that. Becky roused up from her lethargy of distress and showed good interest in the proceedings. She did not expect that Tom could get out of his trouble by denying that he spilled the ink himself; and she was right. The denial only seemed to make the thing worse for Tom. Becky tried to believe she was glad of it, but she found she was not certain. When the worst came to the worst, she had an impulse to get up and tell on Alfred Temple, but she forced herself to keep still—because, said she to herself, he'll tell about me tearing the picture sure. I wouldn't say a word, not to save his life!

Tom took his whipping and went back to his seat not at all brokenhearted, for he thought it was possible that he had unknowingly upset the ink himself, in some skylarking bout—he had denied it for form's sake and because it was custom, and had stuck to the denial from principle.

A whole hour drifted by, the master sat nodding in his throne, the air was drowsy with the hum of study. By and by, Mr. Dobbins straightened himself up, yawned, then unlocked his desk and reached for his book, but seemed undecided whether to take it out or leave it. Most of the pupils glanced up languidly, but there were two among them that watched his movements with intent eyes. Mr. Dobbins fingered his book absently for a while, then took it out and settled himself in his chair to read!

Tom shot a glance at Becky. He had seen a hunted and helpless rabbit look as she did, with a gun leveled at its head. Instantly he forgot his quarrel with her. Quick—something must be done! He would run and snatch the book, spring through the door and fly! But his resolution shook for one little instant, and the chance was lost—the master opened the volume.

The next moment the master faced the school. Every eye sank under his gaze. There was that in it which smote even the innocent with fear. There was silence while one might count ten, the master was gathering his wrath. Then he spoke:

"Who tore this book?"

There was not a sound. One could have heard a pin drop. The master searched face after face for signs of guilt.

"Benjamin Rogers, did you tear this book?"

A denial. A pause.

"Joseph Harper, did you?"

Another denial. Tom's uneasiness grew more and more intense. The master scanned the ranks of boys—considered awhile, then turned to the girls:

"Amy Lawrence?"

A shake of the head.

"Gracie Miller?"

Another negative.

"Rebecca Thatcher [Tom glanced at her face—it was white with terror]—did you tear—no, look me in the face—did you tear this book?"

A thought shot like lightning through Tom's brain. He sprang to his feet and shouted—"*I* done it!"

The school stared in perplexity at this incredible folly. But as Tom stepped forward to go to his punishment the surprise, the gratitude, the adoration that shone upon him out of poor Becky's eyes seemed pay enough for a hundred floggings. Inspired by the splendor of his own act, he took without an outcry the most merciless flaying that even Mr. Dobbins had ever administered; and also received with indifference the added cruelty of a command to remain two hours after school—for he knew who would wait for him outside till his captivity was done.

Tom went to bed that night planning vengeance against Alfred Temple; for with shame and repentance Becky had told him all; but even the longing for vengeance had to give way, soon, to pleasanter musings, and he fell asleep at last, with Becky's latest words lingering dreamily in his ear—

"Tom, how *could* you be so noble!"

VACATION WAS APPROACHING. The schoolmaster, always severe, grew more severe than ever, for he wanted the school to make a good show on Examination Day. His rod and his ferule were seldom idle now. Mr. Dobbins' lashings were very vigorous ones, too; for although he carried, under his wig, a perfectly bald and shiny head, there was no sign of feebleness in his muscle.

As the great day approached, he seemed to take a vindictive pleasure in punishing the least shortcomings. The consequence was that the boys spent their nights in plotting revenge. At last they hit upon a plan that promised victory. They swore in the sign painter's boy, told him the scheme, and asked for his help. He had reasons for being delighted, for the master boarded in his father's family and had given the boy ample cause to hate him. The master always prepared himself for great occasions by getting pretty well fuddled, and when the dominie reached the proper condition on Examination Evening the sign painter's boy said he would "manage the thing" while the master napped in his chair; then he would be awakened at the right time and hurried to school.

In the fullness of time the interesting occasion arrived. At eight in the evening the schoolhouse was brilliantly lighted, and adorned with festoons of flowers. The master sat throned in his chair upon a raised platform, with his blackboard behind him. He was looking tolerably mellow. Rows of benches in front of him were occupied by the dignitaries of the town and by the parents of the pupils. To his left were seated the scholars who were to take part; the rest of the house was filled with nonparticipating scholars.

The exercises began. A very little boy stood up and sheepishly recited, "You'd scarce expect one of my age to speak in public on the stage," etc.—accompanying himself with the painfully exact and spasmodic gestures which a machine might have used—supposing the machine to be a trifle out of order. But he got through safely, though cruelly scared, and got a round of applause.

A little shamefaced girl lisped "Mary had a little lamb," etc., performed a compassion-inspiring curtsy, got her meed of applause and sat down flushed and happy.

Tom Sawyer stepped forward with conceited confidence and soared into the indestructible "Give me liberty or give me death" speech, with fine fury and frantic gesticulation, and broke down in the middle of it. A ghastly stage fright seized him, and his legs quaked. True, he had the manifest sympathy of the house—but he had the house's silence, too, which was even worse than its sympathy. Tom struggled awhile and then retired, utterly defeated. There was a weak attempt at applause, but it died early.

"The Boy Stood on the Burning Deck" followed: also "The Assyrian Came Down," and other declamatory gems. Then there were reading exercises and a spelling fight. The Latin class recited with honor. The feature of the evening was in order now—original "compositions" by the young ladies. Each in her turn stepped forward, cleared her throat, held up her manuscript (tied with dainty ribbon) and proceeded to read, with labored attention to "expression." The themes were the same that had been illuminated by their mothers and grandmothers before them. "Friendship," "Memories of Other Days," "Forms of Political Government Compared and Contrasted," "Melancholy," "Filial Love," etc. It may also be remarked that the number of compositions in which the word "beauteous" was overfondled and human experience referred to as "life's page" was up to the usual average.

When the last composition had been read, the master, mellow almost to the verge of geniality, put his chair aside, turned his back to the audience and began to draw a map of America on the blackboard, to exercise the geography class upon. But he made a sad business of it with his unsteady hand, and a smothered titter rippled over the house. He knew what the matter was and set himself to right it. He sponged out lines and remade them; but the tittering was only more pronounced. He threw his entire attention upon his work, now, as if determined not to be put down by the mirth. Yet the tittering continued; it even manifestly increased.

And well it might. There was a garret above, pierced with a scuttle over his head; and down through this scuttle came a cat, suspended around the haunches by a string; she had a rag tied about her head and jaws to keep her from mewing; as she slowly descended she curved upward and clawed at the string, she swung downward and clawed at the intangible air.

The tittering rose higher and higher—the cat was within six inches of the absorbed teacher's head—down, down, a little lower, and she grabbed his wig with her desperate claws, clung to it, and was snatched up into the garret in an instant with her trophy still in her possession! And how the light did blaze abroad from the master's bald pate—for the sign painter's boy had *gilded* it!

That broke up the meeting. The boys were avenged. Vacation had come.

CHAPTER XI

TOM PRESENTLY WONDERED to find that his coveted vacation was beginning to hang heavily on his hands. Becky Thatcher was gone to her Constantinople home to stay with her parents during vacation—so there was no bright side to life anywhere.

The dreadful secret of the murder was a chronic misery.

Tom attempted a diary—but nothing happened during three days, and so he abandoned it.

Even the Glorious Fourth was in some sense a failure, for it rained hard, and there was no procession in consequence.

Then came the measles.

During two long weeks Tom lay a prisoner. He was very ill, he was interested in nothing. When he got upon his feet at last and moved feebly downtown, a melancholy change had come over everything and every creature. There had been a "revival," and everybody had "got religion." Tom found Joe Harper studying a Testament, and turned sadly away. He sought Ben Rogers, and found him visiting the poor with a basket of tracts. And when, in desperation, he flew for refuge to Huckleberry Finn and was received with a scriptural quotation, his heart broke and he crept home realizing that he alone of all the town was lost forever.

The next day the doctors were back; Tom had relapsed. The three weeks he spent on his back this time seemed an entire age. When he got abroad at last he was hardly grateful that he had been spared, remembering how companionless and forlorn he was. He drifted listlessly down the street and found Joe Harper and Huck Finn up an alley eating a stolen melon. Poor lads! They—like Tom—had suffered a relapse.

Then at last the sleepy atmosphere was stirred—and vigorously: the murder trial came on in the court.

The murder became the absorbing topic of village talk immediately. Tom could not get away from it. Every reference sent a shudder to his heart; he did not see how he could be suspected of knowing anything about the murder, but still he could not be comfortable in the midst of the gossip. It kept him in a cold shiver all the time. He took Huck to a lonely place to have a talk with him. It would be some relief to divide his burden of distress with another sufferer. Moreover, he wanted to assure himself that Huck had remained discreet.

"Huck, have you ever told anybody about—that?"

"Course I haven't. What makes you ask?"

"Well, I was afeard."

"Why, Tom Sawyer, we wouldn't be alive two days if that got found out. *You* know that."

Tom felt more comfortable. After a pause: "Huck, they couldn't anybody get me to tell."

"Well, that's all right, then. I reckon we're safe as long as we keep mum. But let's swear again, anyway. It's more surer."

"I'm agreed."

So they swore again with dread solemnities.

"What is the talk around you, Huck? I've heard a power of it."

"Talk? It's just Muff Potter, Muff Potter all the time. It keeps me in a sweat, constant, so's I want to hide som'ers."

"That's just the same way they go on round me. I reckon he's a goner. Don't you feel sorry for him, sometimes?"

"Most always. He ain't no account; but then he hain't ever done anything to hurt anybody. Just fishes a little, to get money to get drunk on—and loafs. But he give me half a fish, once, when there warn't enough for two; and lots of times he's kind of stood by me when I was out of luck."

"Well, he's mended kites for me, Huck, and knitted hooks onto my line. I wish we could get him out of there."

"My! We couldn't get him out, Tom. And besides, 'twouldn't do any good; they'd ketch him again."

"Yes, they would. But I hate to hear 'em abuse him so like the dickens when he never done—that."

"I do too, Tom. Lord, I hear 'em say he's the bloodiest-looking villain in this country, and they wonder he wasn't ever hung before."

The boys' talk brought them little comfort. As the twilight drew on, they did as they had often done before—went to the cell grating of the little isolated jail and gave Potter some tobacco and matches. His gratitude for their gifts had always smote their conscience before—it cut deeper than ever, this time. They felt cowardly and treacherous to the last degree when Potter said:

"You've been mighty good to me, boys—better'n anybody else in this town. And I don't forget it. Often I says to myself, says I, 'I used to mend all the boys' kites and things, and now they've all forgot old Muff when he's in trouble; but Tom don't, and Huck don't—*they* don't forget him,' says I, 'and I don't forget them.' Well, boys, I done an awful thing—drunk and crazy at the time—and now I got to swing for it, and it's right, I reckon—hope so, anyway. Well, we won't talk about that. Stand a little furder west—so—that's it; it's a prime comfort to see faces that's friendly. Git up on one another's backs and let me shake hands—that's it—yourn'll come through the bars, but mine's too big. Little hands, and weak—but they've helped Muff Potter a power, and they'd help him more if they could."

Tom went home miserable, and his dreams that night were full of horrors. The next day and the day after, he hung about the courtroom, drawn by an almost irresistible impulse to go in, but forcing himself to stay out. Huck was having the same experience. They studiously avoided each other. Tom kept his ears open, but invariably heard distressing news—the toils were closing relentlessly around poor Potter. At the end of the second day the village talk was to the effect that Injun Joe's evidence stood firm and unshaken, and that there was not the slightest question as to what the jury's verdict would be.

All the village flocked to the courthouse on the third morning, for this was to be the great day. After a long wait the jury filed in; shortly afterward, Potter, pale, timid and hopeless, was brought in, with chains upon him, and seated where all the curious could stare at him; no less conspicuous was Injun Joe, stolid as ever. There was another pause, and then the Judge arrived and the sheriff proclaimed the opening of the court.

Now a witness was called who testified that he found Muff Potter washing in a brook, at an early hour of the morning the murder was discovered, and that he immediately sneaked away. After some further questioning, counsel for the prosecution said, "Take the witness."

The prisoner raised his eyes for a moment, but dropped them again when his own counsel said, "I have no questions to ask him."

The next witness proved the finding of the knife near the corpse. Counsel for the prosecution said, "Take the witness."

"I have no questions to ask him," Potter's lawyer replied.

A third witness swore he had often seen the knife in Potter's possession. Again counsel for Potter declined to question. The faces of the audience began to betray annoyance. Did this attorney mean to throw away his client's life without an effort?

Several witnesses deposed concerning Potter's guilty behavior when brought to the scene of the murder. They were allowed to leave the stand without being cross-questioned. The perplexity and dissatisfaction of the house expressed itself in murmurs and provoked a reproof from the bench. Counsel for the prosecution now said, "By the oaths of citizens whose word is above suspicion, we have fastened this awful crime, beyond all possibility of question, upon the unhappy prisoner at the bar. We rest our case here."

A groan escaped from poor Potter, and he put his face in his hands and rocked his body softly to and fro. Many men in the courtroom were moved, and many women's compassion testified itself in tears. Counsel for the defense rose and said:

"Your Honor, in our remarks at the opening of this trial, we foreshadowed our purpose to prove that our client did this fearful deed while under the influence of a blind and irresponsible delirium produced by drink. We have changed our mind. We shall not offer that plea." Then to the clerk: "Call Thomas Sawyer!"

A puzzled amazement awoke in every face in the house, not even excepting Potter's. Every eye fastened itself upon Tom as he took his place upon the stand. The boy looked wild enough, for he was badly scared. The oath was administered.

"Thomas Sawyer, where were you on the seventeenth of June, about the hour of midnight?"

Tom glanced at Injun Joe's iron face and his tongue failed him. The audience listened, breathless, but the words refused to come. After a few moments, however, the boy managed to make part of the house hear:

"In the graveyard!"

"A little louder, please. Don't be afraid. You were—"

"In the graveyard."

A contemptuous smile flitted across Injun Joe's face.

"Were you anywhere near Horse Williams' grave?"

"Yes, sir."

"Speak up—just a trifle louder. How near were you?"

"Near as I am to you."

"Were you hidden, or not?"

"I was hid."

"Where?"

"Behind the trees that's on the edge of the grave."

Injun Joe gave a barely perceptible start.

"Anyone with you?"

"Yes, sir. I went there with—"

"Wait—wait a moment. Never mind mentioning your companion's name. We will produce him at the proper time. Did you carry anything there with you?"

Tom hesitated and looked confused.

"Speak out, my boy. What did you take there?"

"Only a—a—dead cat."

There was a ripple of mirth, which the court checked.

"We will produce the skeleton of that cat. Now, my boy, tell us everything that occurred—in your own way; don't be afraid."

Tom began—hesitatingly at first, but as he warmed to his subject his words flowed more easily; every sound ceased but his own voice, and with bated breath the audience hung upon his words, rapt in the ghastly fascinations of the tale. The strain upon pent emotion reached its climax when the boy said:

"—and as the doctor fetched the board around and Muff Potter fell, Injun Joe jumped with the knife and—"

Crash! Quick as lightning the half-breed sprang for a window, tore his way through all opposers, and was gone!

CHAPTER XII

TOM WAS A GLITTERING HERO once more—the pet of the old, the envy of the young. His name even went into immortal print, for the village paper magnified him. There were some that believed he would be President, yet, if he escaped hanging.

As usual, the fickle, unreasoning world took Muff Potter to its bosom and fondled him as lavishly as it had abused him before. But that sort of conduct is to the world's credit; therefore it is not well to find fault with it.

Tom's days were days of splendor to him, but his nights were seasons of horror. Injun Joe infested all his dreams, and always with doom in his eye. Hardly any temptation could persuade the boy to stir abroad after nightfall. Poor Huck was in the same state, for Tom had told the whole story to Muff Potter's lawyer, and Huck was sore afraid that his share in the business might leak out yet, notwithstanding Injun Joe's flight had saved him the suffering of testifying in court. He had got the attorney to promise secrecy, but what of that? Since Tom's harassed conscience had managed to drive him to the lawyer's house and wring a dread tale from lips that had been sealed with the dismalest of oaths, Huck's confidence in the human race was well-nigh obliterated.

Rewards had been offered, the country had been scoured, but no Injun Joe was found. Half the time Tom was afraid Injun Joe would never be captured; the other half he was afraid he would be. He felt sure he never could draw a safe breath again until that man was dead and he had seen the corpse.

The slow days drifted on, and each left behind it a slightly lightened weight of apprehension.

Meanwhile, one day, Tom found himself with a sudden raging desire to go somewhere and dig for hidden treasure. This desire is one which usually comes at some time or other in every rightly constructed boy's life. He sallied out to find Huck Finn the Red-Handed, and opened the matter to him. Huck was willing. "Where'll we dig?" said Huck.

"Oh, most anywhere."

"Why, is it hid all around?"

"No indeed it ain't. It's hid in mighty particular places—sometimes on islands, sometimes in rotten chests under the end of a limb of an old dead tree, just where the shadow falls at midnight; but mostly under the floor in ha'nted houses."

"Who hides it?" Huck asked.

"Why, robbers, of course—who'd you reckon? Sunday-school sup'rintendents?"

"I don't know. If 'twas mine I wouldn't hide it; I'd spend it."

"So would I. But robbers don't do that way. They always hide it. They think they will come after it, but they generally forget the marks, or else they die. Anyway, it lays there a long time and gets rusty; and by and by somebody finds an old yellow paper that tells how to find the marks—a paper that's got to be ciphered over about a week because it's mostly hi'roglyphics."

"Hiro—which?"

"Hi'roglyphics—pictures and things, you know, that don't seem to mean anything."

"Have you got one of them papers, Tom?"

"No."

"Well then, how you going to find the marks?"

"I don't want any marks. We've tried Jackson's Island a little, and we can try it again; and there's the old ha'nted house up the Still-House branch, and there's lots of dead-limb trees—dead loads of 'em."

"How you going to know which one to go for?"

"Go for all of 'em!"

"Why, Tom, it'll take all summer."

"Well, what of that? Suppose you find a brass pot with a hundred dollars, or a rotten chest full of di'monds. How's that?"

Huck's eyes glowed. "That's bully. Just you gimme the hundred dollars and I don't want no di'monds."

"All right. But I bet you *I* ain't going to throw off on di'monds. Some of 'em's worth twenty dollars apiece—there ain't any, hardly, but's worth six bits or a dollar. Kings have slathers of them."

"Well, all right. But say, Tom—where you going to dig first?"

"S'pose we tackle that old dead-limb tree on the hill t'other side of Still-House branch?"

"I'm agreed."

So they got a crippled pick and a shovel, and set out on their three-mile tramp. They arrived hot and panting, and threw themselves down in the shade of a neighboring elm to rest.

"Say, Huck," said Tom, "if we find a treasure here, what you going to do with your share?"

"Well, I'll have pie and a glass of soda every day, and I'll go to every circus that comes along. I'll have a gay time."

"Ain't you going to save any of it?"

"Save it? What for?"

"Why, so as to have something to live on, by and by."

"Oh, that ain't any use. Pap would come back to town someday and get his claws on it, and I tell you he'd clean it out pretty quick. What you going to do with yourn, Tom?"

"I'm going to buy a new drum, and a sword, and a red necktie and a bull pup, and get married."

"Married! Tom, you—why, you ain't in your right mind! Look at Pap and my mother. Fight! Why, they used to fight all the time."

"That ain't anything. The girl I'm going to marry won't fight."

"Tom, they're all alike. They'll all comb a body. Now you better think 'bout this awhile. What's the name of the gal?"

"I'll tell you sometime—not now."

"All right. Only if you get married I'll be more lonesomer than ever."

"No you won't. You'll come and live with me. Now stir out of this and we'll go to digging."

They worked and sweated for half an hour. No result. They toiled another half hour. Still no result. Huck said, "Do they always bury it as deep as this?"

"Not generally. I reckon we haven't got the right place."

So they chose a new spot and began again. After some time Huck leaned on his shovel, swabbed his brow with his sleeve, and said, "Where you going to dig next, after we get this one?"

"I reckon maybe we'll tackle the old tree that's over yonder on Cardiff Hill back of the widow's."

"I reckon that'll be a good one." The work went on. By and by Huck said, "Blame it, we must be in the wrong place again."

"It *is* mighty curious, Huck. I don't understand it. Oh, *I* know! What blamed fools we are! You got to find out where the shadow of the limb falls at midnight, and that's where you dig!"

"Then confound it, we got to come back in the night. Can you get out?"

"I bet I will."

"Well, I'll come around and meow tonight."

"All right."

That night, about the appointed time, they sat in the shadow waiting. Spirits whispered in the rustling leaves, ghosts lurked in the murky nooks, and the deep baying of a hound floated up out of the distance. The boys talked little. By and by they judged that twelve had come; they marked where the shadow fell, and began to dig. Their hopes commenced to rise, and their interest grew stronger. The hole deepened, but every time their hearts jumped to hear the pick strike something, they suffered a new disappointment. At last Tom said, "It ain't any use, Huck, we're wrong again."

"We *can't* be wrong. We spotted the shadder to a dot."

"I know it, but we only guessed at the time. Like enough it was too late or too early."

Huck dropped his shovel. "That's the very trouble," he said. "We can't ever tell the right time, and besides, I been creeping all over, ever since I got here. Let's try somewheres else."

Tom considered awhile, and then said, "The ha'nted house. That's it!"

"Blame it, I don't like ha'nted houses. Those ghosts come sliding around in a shroud, when you ain't noticing, and peep over your shoulder and grit their teeth. I couldn't stand such a thing, Tom."

"Yes, but, Huck, ghosts don't travel around except at night. They won't hender us from digging there in the daytime."

"Well, that's so. But you know mighty well people don't go about that ha'nted house in the day nor the night."

"Well, nothing's ever been seen in that house except in the night—just blue lights slipping by the windows—no regular ghosts."

"Well, where you see one of them blue lights flickering around, Tom, you can bet there's a ghost mighty close behind it. *You* know that they don't anybody but ghosts use 'em."

"Yes, that's so. But anyway they don't come around in the day-time, so what's the use of our being afeard?"

"Well, all right. We'll tackle the ha'nted house if you say so—but I reckon it's taking chances. Let's hide the tools in the bushes."

They had started down the hill by this time. There in the middle of the moonlit valley below them stood the "ha'nted" house, utterly isolated, its fences gone long ago, rank weeds smothering the doorsteps, a corner of the roof caved in. The boys gazed awhile, half expecting to see a blue light flit past a window; then they struck far off to the right, to give the haunted house a wide berth, and took their way homeward through the woods that adorned the rearward side of Cardiff Hill.

About noon the next day the boys arrived at the dead tree; they had come for their tools. Tom was impatient to go to the haunted house; Huck was also—but suddenly said, "Looky here, Tom, do you know what day it is?"

Tom was startled. "My! I never thought of it, Huck!"

"Well, I didn't neither, but all at once it popped onto me that it was Friday."

"Blame it, a body can't be too careful, Huck. We might 'a' got into an awful scrape, tackling such a thing on a Friday."

"*Might!* Better say we *would!* There's some lucky days, maybe, but Friday ain't."

"Well, Huck, we'll drop this thing for today, and play. Do you know Robin Hood?"

"No. Who's Robin Hood?"

"Why, he was one of the greatest men that was ever in England. He was a robber. He robbed sheriffs and rich people and such like. But he never bothered the poor. He always divided up with 'em."

"Well, he must 'a' been a brick."

"I bet you he was, Huck. He could lick any man in England; and he could take his yew bow and plug a ten-cent piece at a mile and a half. We'll play Robin Hood—it's nobby fun. I'll learn you."

"I'm agreed."

So they played Robin Hood all afternoon, now and then casting an eye down upon the haunted house and passing a remark about the morrow's prospects there. As the sun began to sink into the west they took their way homeward. On Saturday, shortly after noon, they were back. They dug a little in their last hole at the dead tree, not with great hope, but merely because Tom said there were so many cases where people had given up a treasure after getting down within six inches of it, and then somebody else had turned it up with a single thrust of a shovel. The thing failed this time, however, so the boys shouldered their tools and went away feeling that they had fulfilled all the requirements that belong to the business of treasure hunting.

When they reached the haunted house there was something so

weird and grisly about the dead silence that reigned there under the baking sun that they were afraid, for a moment, to venture in. Then they crept to the door and took a trembling peep. They saw a weed-grown, floorless room, an ancient fireplace, vacant windows, a ruinous staircase; and everywhere hung ragged and abandoned cobwebs.

They presently entered, softly, with quickened pulses and muscles tense and ready for instant retreat. In a little while familiarity modified their fears and they gave the place an interested examination, rather wondering at their own boldness. Next they wanted to look upstairs. This was something like cutting off retreat, but they got to daring each other, and of course there could be but one result—they threw their tools into a corner and made the ascent. Up there were the same signs of decay. In one corner they found a closet that promised mystery, but there was nothing in it. Their courage was up now and well in hand. They were about to go down and begin work when—

"Sh!" said Tom.

"What is it?" whispered Huck, blanching with fright.

"Sh! . . . There! . . . Hear it?"

"Yes! . . . Oh, my! Let's run!"

"Keep still! They're coming right toward the door."

The boys stretched themselves upon the floor with their eyes to knotholes, and lay waiting, in a misery of fear.

"They've stopped . . . no—coming . . . here they are. Don't whisper another word, Huck. My, I wish I was out of this!"

Two men entered. Each boy said to himself, There's the old deaf and dumb Spaniard that's been about town once or twice lately—never saw t'other man before.

"T'other" was a ragged, unkempt creature, with nothing very pleasant in his face. The Spaniard was wrapped in a serape; he had bushy white whiskers; long white hair flowed from under his sombrero, and he wore green goggles. When they came in, "t'other" was talking in a low voice; they sat down on the ground, with their backs to the wall, and the speaker's words became more distinct.

"No," said he, "I don't like it. It's dangerous."

"Dangerous!" grunted the "deaf and dumb" Spaniard to the vast surprise of the boys. "Milksop!"

This voice made the boys gasp and quake. It was Injun Joe's! After a silence Joe said, "What's any more dangerous than that job up yonder—but nothing's come of it."

"That's different. Not another house about."

"Well, what's more dangerous than coming here in the daytime! Anybody would suspicion us that saw us."

"*I* know that. But there warn't any other place as handy. I want to quit this shanty. I wanted to yesterday, only it warn't any use trying to stir out of here with those infernal boys playing over there on the hill right in full view."

"Those infernal boys" quaked again, and thought how lucky it was that they had remembered it was Friday and concluded to wait a day. They wished in their hearts they had waited a year.

The two men got out some food and made a luncheon. After a long and thoughtful silence, Injun Joe said, "Look here, lad—you go back up the river where you belong. Wait there till you hear from me. I'll take the chances on dropping into this town just once more. We'll do that 'dangerous' job after I've spied around a little and think things look right for it. Then for Texas! We'll leg it, together!"

This was satisfactory. Both men presently fell to yawning, and Injun Joe said, "I'm dead for sleep! It's your turn to watch."

He curled down in the weeds and soon began to snore. His comrade became quiet and presently began to nod; his head dropped lower, and now both men were snoring. The boys drew a long breath. Tom whispered, "Now's our chance—come!"

Huck said, "I can't—I'd die if they was to wake."

Tom urged—Huck held back. At last Tom started alone. But the first step he made wrung such a hideous creak from the floor that he sank down almost dead with fright. He never made a second attempt. The boys lay there counting the dragging moments till it seemed to them that time must be done and eternity growing gray; and then they were grateful to note that at last the sun was setting.

Now one snore ceased. Injun Joe sat up, stared around, stirred his comrade with his foot and said, "Here! *You're* a watchman, ain't you! All right, though—nothing's happened."

"My! Have I been asleep?"

"Oh, partly, partly. Nearly time for us to be moving, pard. What'll we do with what little swag we've got left?"

"Leave it here, I reckon. No use to take it away till we start south. Six hundred and fifty in silver's something to carry."

"Yes, but look here; it may be a good while before I get the right chance at that job; accidents might happen; 'tain't in such a very good place; we'll just regularly bury it."

"Good idea," said the comrade, who walked across the room, knelt down, raised one of the hearthstones and took out a bag that jingled pleasantly. He subtracted from it twenty or thirty dollars for himself and as much for Injun Joe and passed the bag to the latter, who was in the corner, now, digging with his bowie knife.

The boys forgot all their fears in an instant. With gloating eyes they watched every movement. Luck! The splendor of it was beyond imagination! Six hundred dollars was money enough to make half a dozen boys rich! Here was treasure-hunting under the happiest auspices—there would not be any bothersome uncertainty as to where to dig. They nudged each other every moment—eloquent nudges easily understood, for they simply meant—Oh, but ain't you glad *now* we're here!

Joe's knife struck upon something. "Hello!" said he.

"What is it?" said his comrade.

"Half-rotten plank—no, it's a box! Here—I've broke a hole." He reached his hand in. "Man, it's money!"

The two men examined the handful of coins. They were gold. The boys above were as excited as themselves, and as delighted.

Joe's comrade said, "We'll make quick work of this. There's an old rusty pick over in that corner—I saw it a minute ago."

He brought the boys' pick and shovel. Injun Joe took the pick, looked it over critically, shook his head, and then began to use it. The ironbound box was soon unearthed. The men contemplated the treasure in it.

"Pard, there's thousands of dollars here," said Injun Joe.

"'Twas always said that Murrel's gang used to be around here one summer," the stranger observed.

"I know it," said Injun Joe; "and this looks like it."

"*Now* you won't need to do that job."

The half-breed frowned. Said he, "You don't know all about that thing. 'Tain't robbery—it's *revenge!*" and a wicked light flamed in his eyes. "I'll need your help in it. When it's finished—then Texas. Go home to your Nance and your kids, and stand by till you hear from me."

"Well—if you say so. What'll we do with this—bury it again?"

"Yes. [Ravishing delight overhead.] *No!* By the great Sachem, no! [Profound distress overhead.] I'd nearly forgot. That pick had fresh earth on it! [The boys were sick with terror in a moment.] What business has a pick and shovel here? Who brought them here—and where are they gone? What! Bury it again and leave them to come and see the ground disturbed? Not exactly. We'll take it to my den."

"Why, of course! You mean Number One?"

"No—Number Two—under the cross. The other place is too common."

"All right. It's nearly dark enough to start."

Injun Joe got up and went about from window to window peeping out. Presently he said, "Who could have brought those tools here? Do you reckon they can be upstairs?"

The boys' breath forsook them. Injun Joe put his hand on his knife, halted a moment, undecided, and then turned toward the stairway. The boys thought of the closet, but their strength was gone. The steps came creaking up the stairs—the intolerable distress of the situation woke the stricken resolution of the lads—they were about to spring for the closet, when there was a crash of rotten timbers and Injun Joe landed on the ground amid the debris of the ruined stairway. He gathered himself up cursing, and his comrade said:

"Now what's the use of all that? If anybody's up there, let them *stay* there—who cares? If they want to jump down, now, and get into trouble, who objects? It will be dark in fifteen minutes—and then let them follow us if they want to. In my opinion, whoever hove those things in here caught a sight of us and took us for ghosts or something. I'll bet they're running yet."

Joe grumbled awhile; then he agreed with his friend. Shortly afterward they slipped out of the house in the twilight, and moved toward the river with their precious box.

Tom and Huck rose up, weak but vastly relieved, and stared after them through the chinks between the logs of the house. Follow? Not they. They were content to reach ground again without broken necks, and take the townward track over the hill. They did not talk much. They were too much absorbed in hating themselves—hating the ill luck that made them take the spade and the pick there. But for that, Injun Joe never would have suspected. He would have hidden the silver with the gold to wait there till his "revenge" was satisfied, and then he would have had the misfortune to find that money turn up missing.

They resolved to keep a lookout for that Spaniard when he should come to town spying out for chances to do his revengeful job, and follow him to "Number Two," wherever that might be. Then a ghastly thought occurred to Tom. "Revenge. What if he means *us*, Huck!"

"Oh, don't!" said Huck, nearly fainting.

They talked it all over, and as they entered town they agreed to believe that he might possibly mean somebody else—might at least mean nobody but Tom, since only Tom had testified.

Very, very small comfort it was to Tom to be alone in danger! Company would be a palpable improvement, he thought.

CHAPTER XIII

THE ADVENTURE OF THE DAY mightily tormented Tom's dreams that night. In the morning it even occurred to him that the great adventure itself might have been a dream! There was one very strong argument in favor of this idea—namely, that the quantity of coin he had seen was too vast to be real. He had never seen as much as fifty dollars in one mass before, and he was like all boys of his age and station in life, in that he imagined that all references to "hundreds" and "thousands" were mere fanciful forms of speech, and that no such sums really existed in the world. This uncertainty must be swept away. He snatched a hurried breakfast and went to find Huck. Huck was sitting on the gunwale of a flatboat, dangling his feet in the water and looking very melancholy.

"Hello, Huck!"

"Hello, yourself." Silence for a minute. "Tom, if we'd 'a' left the blame tools at the dead tree, we'd 'a' got the money. Oh, ain't it awful!"

"'Tain't a dream, then! Somehow I most wish it was."

"What ain't a dream?"

"That thing yesterday."

"Dream! If them stairs hadn't broke down you'd 'a' seen how much dream it was! I've had dreams enough all night—with that patch-eyed Spanish devil going for me all through 'em—rot him!"

"No, not rot him. *Find* him! Track the money!"

"Tom, we'll never find him. A feller don't have only one chance for such a pile—and that one's lost. I'd feel mighty shaky if I was to see him, anyway."

"Well, so'd I; but I'd like to see him, anyway—and track him out—to his Number Two."

"Number Two—yes. I ben thinking 'bout that. What do you reckon it is?"

"I dono. Say, Huck—maybe it's the number of a house!"

"Goody! . . . No, Tom, that ain't it. If it is, it ain't in this one-horse town. They ain't no numbers here."

"Well, that's so. Lemme think a minute. Here—the number of a room—in a tavern?"

"Oh, that's the trick! They ain't only two taverns. We can find out quick."

"You stay here, Huck, till I come."

Tom was off at once, and was gone half an hour. He found that in the best tavern, Number Two had long been occupied by a young lawyer. In the less ostentatious Temperance Tavern,

Number Two was a mystery. The tavern keeper's young son said it was kept locked all the time, and he never saw anybody go in or out of it except at night; he did not know any particular reason for this; had had some curiosity, but had entertained himself with the idea that room was "ha'nted."

"That's what I've found out, Huck. I reckon that's the very Number Two we're after."

"I reckon it is, Tom. Now what you going to do?"

Tom thought. Then he said, "I'll tell you. The back door of that Number Two comes out into that little close alley between the tavern and the old brick store. Now you get hold of all the door keys you can find, and I'll nip all of Auntie's, and the first dark night we'll go there and try 'em. And mind you, keep a lookout for Injun Joe, because he said he was going to drop into town once more. If you see him, you just follow him; and if he don't go to that Number Two, that ain't the place."

"Lordy, I don't want to foller him by myself!"

"Why, it'll be night, sure. He mightn't ever see you—and if he did, maybe he'd never think anything."

"Well, I dono. If it's pretty dark—I'll try."

"You bet *I'll* follow him, if it's dark, Huck. Why, he might 'a' found out he couldn't get his revenge, and be going right after that money."

"It's so, Tom. I'll foller him; I will, by jingos!"

"Now you're *talking!* Don't you weaken, Huck, and I won't."

THAT NIGHT TOM AND HUCK were ready for their adventure. They hung about the tavern until after nine, one watching the alley and the other the tavern door. Nobody entered the alley or left it; nobody resembling the Spaniard entered or left the tavern door. The night promised to be a fair one; so Tom went home with the understanding that if a considerable degree of darkness came on, Huck was to come and "meow," whereupon he would slip out and try the keys. But the night remained clear, and Huck retired to bed in an empty sugar hogshead about twelve.

Tuesday the boys had the same ill luck. Also Wednesday. But

Thursday night promised better. Tom slipped out with his aunt's old tin lantern, and a large towel to blindfold it with. He hid the lantern in Huck's sugar hogshead and the watch began. An hour before midnight the tavern lights (the only ones thereabouts) were put out. No Spaniard had been seen. Nobody had entered or left the alley. Darkness reigned. Everything was auspicious.

Tom got his lantern, lit it, wrapped it in the towel, and the two adventurers crept in the gloom toward the tavern. Huck stood sentry and Tom felt his way into the alley. Then there was a season of waiting anxiety that weighed upon Huck's spirits like a mountain. Momentarily he expected catastrophe, and it seemed as if his heart would soon wear itself out, the way it was beating. Suddenly there was a flash of light and Tom came tearing by him. "Run!" said he. "Run for your life!"

He needn't have repeated it; once was enough; Huck was making thirty or forty miles an hour before the repetition was uttered. The boys never stopped till they reached the shed of a deserted slaughterhouse at the lower end of the village. As soon as Tom got his breath he said:

"Huck, it was awful! I tried two of the keys, just as soft as I could; but they made a power of racket. They wouldn't turn in the lock, either. Well, without noticing what I was doing, I took hold of the knob, and open comes the door! It warn't locked! I hopped in, and shook off the towel, and, *great Caesar's ghost!*"

"What—what'd you see, Tom?"

"Huck, I most stepped onto Injun Joe's hand! He was laying there, sound asleep on the floor, with his old patch on his eye and his arms spread out."

"Lordy, what did you do? Did he wake up?"

"No, never budged. Drunk, I reckon. I just grabbed that towel and started!"

"I'd never 'a' thought of the towel, I bet!"

"Well, *I* would. My aunt would make me mighty sick if I lost it."

"Say, Tom, did you see that box?"

"Huck, I didn't wait to look around. I didn't see anything but a bottle and a tin cup on the floor by Injun Joe; yes, and I saw two barrels and lots more bottles. Don't you see, now, what's the matter with that ha'nted room?"

"How?"

"Why, it's ha'nted with whiskey! Maybe *all* the Temperance Taverns have got a ha'nted room, hey, Huck?"

"I reckon maybe that's so. Who'd 'a' thought such a thing? But say, Tom, now's a mighty good time to get that box, if Injun Joe's drunk."

"It is that! You try it!"

Huck shuddered. "Well, no—I reckon not."

"Only one bottle alongside of Injun Joe ain't enough, Huck. If there'd been three, he'd be drunk enough and I'd do it."

There was a long pause for reflection, and then Tom said, "Looky here, Huck, let's not try that thing anymore till we know Injun Joe's not in there. Now, if we watch every night, we'll be dead sure to see him go out, sometime or other, and then we'll snatch that box quicker'n lightning."

"Well, I'm agreed. I'll watch the whole night long, and I'll do it every night, too, if you'll do the other part of the job."

"All right, I will. All you got to do is to trot up Hooper Street a block and meow."

"Agreed, and good as wheat!"

"Now, Huck, I'll go home. It'll begin to be daylight in a couple of hours. You go back and watch, will you?"

"I'll ha'nt that tavern every night for a year, Tom! I'll sleep all day and I'll stand watch all night."

"That's all right. Now, where you going to sleep?"

"In Ben Rogers' hayloft."

"Well, if I don't want you in the daytime, I'll let you sleep. I won't come bothering around. Anytime you see something's up, in the night, just skip right around and meow."

THE FIRST THING TOM HEARD on Friday morning was a glad piece of news—Judge Thatcher's family had come back to town. Both Injun Joe and the treasure sank into secondary importance for a moment, and Becky took the chief place in the boy's interest. He saw her, and they had an exhausting good time playing "hi-spy" and "gully-keeper" with a crowd of their schoolmates.

The day was crowned in a peculiarly satisfactory way: Becky teased her mother to appoint the next day for the long-promised picnic, and she consented. The invitations were sent out before sunset, and straightway the young folks of the village were thrown into a fever of pleasurable anticipation. Tom's excitement enabled him to keep awake until a late hour, and he had good hopes of hearing Huck's "meow," and of having his treasure to astonish Becky and the picnickers with, next day; but he was disappointed; no signal came that night.

Morning came, eventually, and by eleven o'clock a giddy and rollicking company were gathered at Judge Thatcher's. It was not the custom for elderly people to mar picnics with their presence. The children were considered safe enough under the wings of a few young ladies of eighteen and a few young gentlemen of twenty-three or thereabouts. The old steam ferryboat was chartered for the occasion; presently the gay throng filed up the main street laden with provision baskets. Sid was sick and had to miss the fun; Mary remained at home to entertain him. The last thing Mrs. Thatcher said to Becky was, "You'll not get back till late. Perhaps you'd better stay all night with one of the girls that live near the ferry landing, child."

"Then I'll stay with Susy Harper, Mamma."

"Very well. Mind and behave yourself."

Three miles below town the ferryboat stopped at the mouth of a woody hollow and tied up. The crowd swarmed ashore and soon the forest distances and craggy heights echoed with shoutings and laughter. All the different ways of getting hot and tired were gone through with, and by and by the rovers straggled back to camp fortified with responsible appetites, and then the destruction of the good things began. After the feast there was a refreshing season of rest and chat in the shade. By and by somebody shouted, "Who's ready for the cave?"

Everybody was. Candles were procured, and straightway there

was a general scamper up the hill. The mouth of the cave was up the hillside—an opening shaped like a letter A. Its massive oaken door stood unbarred. Within was a small chamber, chilly as an icehouse, and walled with limestone that was dewy with a cold sweat.

It was romantic and mysterious to stand here in the gloom and look out upon the green valley shining in the sun. But the impressiveness of the situation quickly wore off, and the romping began again. By and by the procession went filing down the steep descent of the main avenue, the flickering rank of lights dimly revealing the lofty walls of rock almost to their point of junction sixty feet overhead. This main avenue was not more than eight or ten feet wide.

Every few steps other lofty and still narrower crevices branched from it on either hand—for McDougal's Cave was but a vast labyrinth of crooked aisles that ran into each other and out again and led nowhere. It was said that one might wander days and nights together through its tangle of rifts and chasms, and never find the end; and that he might go down and down, into the earth, and it was just the same—labyrinth underneath labyrinth, and no end to any of them. No man "knew" the cave. Most of the young men knew a portion of it, and it was not customary to venture much beyond this known portion. Tom Sawyer knew as much of the cave as anyone.

The procession moved along the main avenue some three quarters of a mile, and then groups and couples began to slip aside into branch avenues, fly along the dismal corridors, and take each other by surprise at points where the corridors joined again. Parties were able to elude each other for the space of half an hour without going beyond the "known" ground.

By and by, one group after another came straggling back to the mouth of the cave, panting, hilarious, smeared with tallow drippings and daubed with clay. Then they were astonished to find that they had been taking no note of time and that night was at hand. The clanging bell had been calling for half an hour. However, this sort of close to the day's adventures was romantic and therefore satisfactory. When the ferryboat with her wild freight pushed into the stream, nobody cared sixpence for the wasted time but the captain of the craft.

Huck was already upon his watch when the ferryboat's lights went past the wharf. He heard no noise on board, for the young people were as subdued as people usually are who are nearly tired to death. He wondered what boat it was, and then he dropped it out of his mind and put his attention upon his business. The night was growing cloudy and dark. Ten o'clock came, and the noise of vehicles ceased, scattered lights began to wink out, the village betook itself to its slumbers and left the small watcher alone with the silence. Eleven o'clock came, and the tavern lights were put out; darkness everywhere, now. Huck waited what seemed a weary long time, but nothing happened. His faith was weakening. Was there any use? Why not give it up and turn in?

A noise fell upon his ear. He was all attention in an instant. The alley door closed softly. He sprang to the corner of the brick store. The next moment two men brushed by him, and one seemed to have something under his arm. It must be that box! So they were going to remove the treasure. Why call Tom now? It would be absurd—the men would get away with the box and never be found again. No, he would follow them; he would trust to the darkness for security from discovery. So Huck stepped out and glided along behind the men, catlike, with bare feet, allowing them to keep just far enough ahead not to be invisible.

They moved up the river street, then turned left and went straight ahead to the path that led up Cardiff Hill. This they took, climbing up toward the summit. Presently they plunged into a narrow path between tall sumac bushes, and were at once hidden in the gloom. Huck shortened his distance, now, for they would never be able to see him. He trotted along awhile; then slackened his pace, fearing he was gaining too fast; then stopped altogether; listened; no sound save the beating of his own heart. The hooting of an owl came from over the hill. But no footsteps. Heavens, was everything lost! He was about to spring with winged feet, when a man cleared his throat not four feet from him! Huck's heart shot into his throat, but he swallowed it again; then he stood there shaking as if a dozen agues had taken charge of him. He knew where he was. He was within five steps of the stile leading into Widow Douglas's grounds. Very well, he thought, let them bury it there; it won't be hard to find.

Now there was a voice—a very low voice—Injun Joe's:

"Damn her, maybe she's got company—there's lights, late as it is."

"I can't see any."

This was the stranger's voice—the stranger of the haunted house. A deadly chill went to Huck's heart—this, then, was the "revenge" job! His thought was to fly. Then he remembered that the Widow Douglas had been kind to him more than once, and maybe these men were going to murder her. He wished he dared venture to warn her; but he didn't dare—they might come and catch him. He thought all this in the moment that elapsed between the stranger's remark and Injun Joe's next—which was—

"Because the bush is in your way. Now—this way—now you see, don't you?"

"Yes. Well, there *is* company, I reckon. Better give it up."

"Give it up, and I just leaving this country forever! Give it up and never have another chance! I tell you, I don't care for her swag—you can have it. But her husband was rough on me many times—he was the justice of the peace that jugged me for a vagrant. And that ain't all. He had me horsewhipped! *Horsewhipped!* In front of the jail—with all the town looking on! Then he took advantage of me and died. But I'll take it out of *her*."

"Oh, don't kill her! Don't do that!"

"Kill? Who said anything about killing? I would kill *him* if he was here, but not her. When you want to get revenge on a woman you don't kill her—bosh! You go for her looks. You slit her nostrils—you notch her ears like a sow!"

"By God, that's—"

"Keep your opinion to yourself! I'll tie her to the bed. If she bleeds to death, is that my fault? You'll help in this thing, my friend, that's why you're here—I mightn't be able alone. If you flinch, I'll kill you. Do you understand?"

"Well, if it's got to be done, let's get at it. The quicker the better—I'm all in a shiver."

"Do it *now?* And company there? No—we'll wait till the lights are out."

Huck held his breath and stepped gingerly back; planted his foot carefully, after balancing, one-legged, in a precarious way and almost toppling over. He took another step back, with the same elaboration and the same risks; then another and another, and—a twig snapped under his foot! His breath stopped and he listened. There was no sound. His gratitude was measureless. Now he turned in his tracks, between the walls of sumac bushes—turned himself as carefully as if he were a ship—and then stepped quickly but cautiously along. When he felt secure he picked up his nimble heels and flew. Down, down he sped, till he reached a house belonging to an old Welshman, halfway down the hill. He banged at the door, and presently the heads of the old man and his two stalwart sons were thrust from windows.

"What's the row there? What do you want?"

"Let me in—quick! It's me—Huckleberry Finn!"

"Huckleberry Finn, indeed! It ain't a name to open many doors! But let him in, lads, and let's see what's the trouble."

"Please don't ever tell *I* told you," were Huck's first words when he got in. "Please don't—I'd be killed, sure—but the widow's been good friends to me, and I want to tell—I *will* tell if you'll promise you won't ever say it was me."

"By George, he *has* got something to tell, or he wouldn't act so!" exclaimed the old man. "Out with it, and nobody here'll ever tell, lad."

Three minutes later the old man and his sons, well armed, were up the hill and entering the sumac path on tiptoe, their weapons in their hands. Huck accompanied them no farther. He hid behind a boulder and fell to listening. There was a lagging, anxious silence, and then all of a sudden there was an explosion of firearms and a cry.

Huck waited for no particulars. He sprang away and sped down the hill as fast as his legs could carry him.

CHAPTER XIV

As the earliest suspicion of dawn appeared on Sunday morning, Huck rapped gently at the old Welshman's door. The inmates were asleep, but it was a sleep that was set on a hair trigger. A call came from a window: "Who's there!"

Huck's scared voice answered, "It's only Huck Finn!"

"It's a name that can open this door night or day, lad—and welcome!"

These were strange words to the vagabond boy's ears. He could not recollect that the closing word had ever been applied in his case before. The door was unlocked, and he entered. He was given a seat, and the old man and his tall sons dressed speedily.

"Now, my boy, I hope you're good and hungry, because breakfast will be ready soon! I and the boys hoped you'd stop here last night."

"I was awful scared," said Huck. "I took out when the pistols went off, and I didn't stop for three mile. I've come now becuz I wanted to know about it, and I come before daylight becuz I didn't want to run acrost them devils, even if they was dead."

"You do look as if you've had a hard night—but there'll be a bed here for you when you've had your breakfast. No, they ain't dead, lad—we are sorry for that. We crept along on tiptoe till we got within fifteen feet of them—dark as a cellar that sumac path was—and just then I found I was going to sneeze. I tried to keep it back, but no use! The sneeze started those scoundrels a-rustling, so I sung out, 'Fire, boys!' and blazed away at the place where the rustling was. So did the boys. But they were off in a jiffy, those villains, and we after them, down through the woods. I judge we never touched them. They fired a shot apiece as they started, but their bullets whizzed by us. As soon as we lost the sound of their feet we went and stirred up the constables. They got a posse together, and went off to guard the riverbank, and as soon as it is light the sheriff and a gang are going to beat up the woods. My boys will be with them presently. I wish we had some sort of description of those rascals. But you couldn't see what they were like in the dark, lad, I suppose?"

"Oh, yes, I saw them downtown and follered them. One's the old deaf and dumb Spaniard that's ben around here once or twice, and t'other's a mean-looking, ragged—"

"That's enough, lad, we know the men! Happened on them in the woods one day, and they slunk away. Boys, tell the sheriff—get your breakfast tomorrow morning!"

The Welshman's sons departed at once. As they were leaving Huck exclaimed, "Oh, please don't tell *anybody* it was me that blowed on them! Oh, please!"

"All right if you say it, Huck, but you ought to have the credit of what you did."

When the young men were gone, the old Welshman said, "They won't tell—and I won't. But how did you come to follow these fellows, lad? Were they looking suspicious?"

Huck was silent while he framed a duly cautious reply. Then he said, "Well, you see, I'm a kind of a hard lot—least everybody says so—and sometimes I can't sleep much on account of thinking about it and sort of trying to strike out a new way of doing. That was the way of it last night. I couldn't sleep, and so I come along up street 'bout midnight, a-turning it all over, and just when I got to that old brick store by the Temperance Tavern along comes these two chaps, slipping along close by me. They had something under their arm, and I reckoned they'd stole it. Then they went on, and I follered 'em. I wanted to see what was up—they sneaked along so. I dogged 'em to the widder's stile, and stood in the dark and heard the ragged one beg for the widder, and the Spaniard swear he'd spile her looks just as I told you and your two—"

"What! The *deaf and dumb* man said all that!"

Huck had made a terrible mistake! He was trying his best to keep the old man from getting the faintest hint of who the Spaniard might be, and yet his tongue seemed determined to get him into trouble. He made several efforts to creep out of his scrape, but the old man's eye was upon him and he made blunder after blunder.

Presently the Welshman said, "My boy, don't be afraid of me. I wouldn't hurt a hair of your head for all the world. You know something about that Spaniard that you want to keep dark. Now tell me what it is, and trust me—I won't betray you."

Huck looked into the old man's honest eyes a moment, then bent over and whispered, "'Tain't a Spaniard—it's Injun Joe!"

The Welshman almost jumped out of his chair. In a moment he said, "It's all plain enough, now. When you talked about notching ears and slitting noses I judged that that was your own embellishment, because white men don't take that sort of revenge. But an Injun! That's a different matter altogether."

During breakfast the talk went on, and in the course of it the old man said that the last thing which he and his sons had done, before going to bed, was to get a lantern and examine the stile and its vicinity for marks of blood. They found none, but captured a bulky bundle of—

"Of WHAT?"

If the words had been lightning they could not have leaped with a more stunning suddenness from Huck's blanched lips. His eyes were staring wide, now, and his breath suspended—waiting for the answer. The Welshman started—stared in return—then replied, "Of burglar's tools. Why, what's the *matter* with you?"

Huck sank back, unutterably grateful. The Welshman eyed him curiously. "That appears to relieve you a good deal. What were *you* expecting we'd found?"

Huck was in a close place—the inquiring eye was upon him—a senseless reply offered—at a venture he uttered it: "Sunday-school books, maybe."

The old man laughed, loud and joyously, and ended by saying that such a laugh was money in a man's pocket, because it cut down the doctor's bills. Then he added, "Poor old chap, you're white and jaded—you ain't well—no wonder you're a little flighty. But rest and sleep will fetch you out all right, I hope."

Huck was irritated to think he had betrayed such a suspicious excitement, for before this he had all but dropped the idea that the parcel brought from the tavern was the treasure. But on the whole he felt glad the little episode had happened, for now he knew beyond all question that that bundle was not *the* bundle, and so his mind was at rest. The treasure must be still in Number Two, the men would be captured and jailed that day, and he and Tom could seize the gold that night without any fear of interruption.

Just as breakfast was completed there was a knock at the door. Huck jumped for a hiding place, for he had no mind to be connected even remotely with the late event. The Welshman admitted several ladies and gentlemen, among them the Widow Douglas, and noticed that groups of citizens were climbing up the hill—to stare at the stile. So the news had spread.

The Welshman had to tell the story of the night to the visitors. He told all, save Huck's role in the affair. The widow's gratitude for her preservation was outspoken. "I went to sleep reading in bed and slept straight through all the noise," she said. "Why didn't you come and wake me?"

"We judged it warn't worthwhile. Those fellows warn't likely to come again—and what was the use of waking you up and scaring you to death? My three Negro men stood guard at your house the rest of the night. They've just come back."

More visitors came, and the story had to be told and retold for a couple of hours more.

There was no Sabbath school during day-school vacation, but everybody was early at church. The stirring event was well canvassed. News came that not a sign of the two villains had been yet discovered. When the sermon was finished, Judge Thatcher's wife dropped alongside of Mrs. Harper as she moved down the aisle with the crowd and said, "Is my Becky going to sleep all day? I just expected she would be tired to death."

"Your Becky?"

"Yes"—with a startled look. "Didn't she stay with you last night?"

"Why, no."

Mrs. Thatcher turned pale, and sank into a pew, just as Aunt Polly passed by. Aunt Polly said, "Good morning, Mrs. Thatcher, Mrs. Harper. I've got a boy that's turned up missing. I reckon my

Tom stayed at your house last night—one of you. And now he's afraid to come to church. I've got to settle with him."

Mrs. Thatcher shook her head and turned paler than ever. "He didn't stay with us," said Mrs. Harper, beginning to look uneasy. A marked anxiety came into Aunt Polly's face.

"Joe Harper, have you seen my Tom this morning?"

"No'm."

"When did you see him last?"

Joe tried to remember, but was not sure he could say. People had stopped moving out of church, and uneasiness took possession of every countenance. Children were anxiously questioned, and young teachers. They all said they had not noticed whether Tom and Becky were on board the ferryboat on the homeward trip; it was dark; no one thought of inquiring if anyone was missing. One young man finally blurted out his fear that they were still in the cave! Mrs. Thatcher swooned away. Aunt Polly fell to crying and wringing her hands.

The alarm swept from lip to lip, from group to group, and within five minutes the bells were wildly clanging and the whole town was up! The widow's burglars were forgotten, horses were saddled, the ferryboat was ordered out, and before the horror was half an hour old two hundred men were pouring down highroad and river toward the cave.

All the long afternoon the village seemed empty and dead. Many women visited Aunt Polly and Mrs. Thatcher and tried to comfort them. All the tedious night the town waited for news; but when the morning dawned at last, all the word that came was, "Send more candles—and send food." Judge Thatcher sent hopeful messages from the cave, but they conveyed no real cheer.

The old Welshman came home toward daylight, spattered with candle grease and worn out. He found Huck still in the bed that he had provided for him, and delirious with fever. The physicians were all at the cave, so the Widow Douglas came and took charge of the patient. Mr. Jones said Huck had good spots in him, and the widow said, "You can depend on it. That's the Lord's mark. He puts it somewhere on every creature that comes from His hands."

Early in the forenoon parties of jaded men began to straggle into the village, but the strongest of the citizens continued searching. All the news that could be gained was that remotenesses of the cavern were being ransacked that had never been visited before; that wherever one wandered through the maze of passages, lights were to be seen flitting hither and thither in the distance, and shoutings and pistol shots sent their hollow reverberations down the somber aisles. In one place, far from the section usually traversed by tourists, the names *Becky & Tom* had been found traced upon the rocky wall with candle smoke, and near at hand a grease-soiled bit of ribbon. Mrs. Thatcher recognized the ribbon and cried over it.

Three dreadful days and nights dragged their tedious hours along, and the village sank into a hopeless stupor. No one had heart for anything. The tremendous discovery, just made, that the proprietor of the Temperance Tavern kept liquor on his premises, scarcely fluttered the public pulse. In a lucid interval, Huck feebly led up to the subject of taverns, and asked—dimly dreading the worst—if anything had been discovered at the Temperance Tavern.

"Yes," said the widow.

Huck started up in bed, wild-eyed. "What! What was it?"

"Liquor! And the place has been shut up. Lie down, child—What a turn you did give me!"

"Only tell me just one thing—just one—please! Was it Tom Sawyer that found it?"

The widow burst into tears. "Hush, child, hush! I've told you before, you must *not* talk. You are very, very sick!"

Then nothing but liquor had been found; there would have been a great powwow if it had been the gold. So the treasure was gone forever—gone forever! But what could she be crying about? These thoughts worked their dim way through Huck's mind, and under the weariness they gave him he fell asleep. The widow said to herself, There—he's asleep, poor wreck. Tom Sawyer find it! Pity but somebody could find Tom Sawyer! Ah, there ain't many left, now, that's got hope enough, or strength enough, either, to go on searching.

CHAPTER XV

Now to return to Tom and Becky's share in the picnic. They tripped along the murky aisles with the rest of the company, visiting the familiar wonders of the cave—wonders dubbed with rather overdescriptive names, such as The Drawing Room, The Cathedral, Aladdin's Palace and so on. Presently the hide-and-seek frolicking began, and Tom and Becky engaged in it with zeal until the exertion began to grow a trifle wearisome; then they wandered down a sinuous avenue holding their candles aloft and reading the tangled webwork of names, dates and mottoes with which the rocky walls had been frescoed (in candle smoke). Still drifting along and talking, they scarcely noticed that they were now in a part of the cave whose walls were not frescoed. They smoked their own names under an overhanging shelf and moved on.

Presently they came to a place where a little stream of water, trickling over a ledge and carrying a limestone sediment with it, had, in the slow-dragging ages, formed a laced and ruffled Niagara in gleaming stone. Tom squeezed his small body behind it in order to illuminate it for Becky's gratification. He found that it curtained a sort of steep natural stairway which was enclosed between narrow walls, and at once the ambition to be a discoverer seized him. Becky responded to his call, and they made a smoke mark for future guidance and started upon their quest. They wound this way and that, far down into the secret depths of the cave, made another mark, and branched off in search of novelties to tell the upper world about. In one place they found a spacious cavern, from whose ceiling depended a multitude of shining stalactites of the length and circumference of a man's leg; they walked all about it, wondering and admiring, and presently left it by one of the numerous passages that opened into it.

This shortly brought them to a cavern whose walls were supported by many fantastic pillars, formed by the joining of great stalactites and stalagmites together. Under the roof vast knots of bats had packed themselves together, thousands in a bunch; the lights disturbed the creatures, and they came flocking down by hundreds, squeaking and darting furiously at the candles. Tom knew their ways and the danger of this sort of conduct. He seized Becky's hand and hurried her into the first corridor that offered; and none too soon, for a bat struck Becky's light out with its wing while she was passing out of the cavern. The bats chased the children a good distance; but the fugitives plunged into every new passage that offered, and at last got rid of the perilous things.

Tom found a subterranean lake, shortly, which stretched its dim length away until its shape was lost in the shadows. He wanted to explore its borders, but concluded that it would be best to sit down and rest awhile, first. Now, for the first time, the deep stillness of the place laid a clammy hand upon the spirits of the children. Becky said, "Why, I didn't notice, but it seems ever so long since I heard any of the others."

"Come to think, Becky, we are away down below them—and I don't know how far away north, or south, or east, or whichever it is. We couldn't hear them here."

Becky grew apprehensive. "I wonder how long we've been down here, Tom. We better start back."

"Yes, I reckon we better."

"Can you find the way, Tom? It's all a mixed-up crookedness to me."

"I reckon I could find it—but then the bats. If they put both our candles out it will be an awful fix. Let's try not to go through there."

They started through a corridor, and traversed it in silence a long way, glancing at each new opening to see if there was anything familiar about the look of it; but they were all strange. Every time Tom made an examination, Becky would watch his face for an encouraging sign, and he would say cheerily, "Oh, it's all right. This ain't the one, but we'll come to it right away!"

But he felt less and less hopeful with each failure, and presently began to turn off into diverging avenues at sheer random. He still said it was "all right," but there was such a leaden dread at his heart that the words had lost their ring and sounded just as if he had said, All is lost! Becky clung to his side in an anguish of fear. At last she said, "Oh, Tom, never mind the bats, let's go back that way! We seem to get worse off all the time."

Tom stopped. "Listen!" said he.

Profound silence; silence so deep that even their breathings were conspicuous. Tom shouted. The call went echoing down the aisles and died out in the distance in a faint sound that resembled a ripple of mocking laughter.

"Oh, don't do it again, Tom, it is too horrid," said Becky.

"It is horrid, but I better, Becky; they *might* hear us, you know," and he shouted again.

The "might" was even a chillier horror than the ghostly laughter, it so confessed a perishing hope. The children stood still and listened; but there was no result. Tom turned upon the back track at once, and hurried his steps. It was but a little while before a certain indecision in his manner revealed another fearful fact to Becky—he could not find his way back!

"Oh, Tom, you didn't make any marks!"

"Becky, I was such a fool! I never thought we might want to come back! No—I can't find the way. It's all mixed up."

"Tom, Tom, we're lost! Oh, why *did* we leave the others!"

She sank to the ground and burst into such a frenzy of crying that Tom was appalled. He sat down by her and put his arms around her; she buried her face in his bosom, she clung to him, she poured out her terrors, and the far echoes turned them all to jeering laughter. Tom begged her to pluck up hope again, and she said she could not. He fell to blaming and abusing himself for getting her into this situation; this had a better effect. She said she would try to hope again, she would get up and follow wherever he might lead if only he would not talk like that anymore. For he was no more to blame than she, she said.

So they moved on again—simply at random. Moving, in some direction, in any direction, might at least bear fruit; to sit down was to invite death. But at last Becky's frail limbs refused to carry her farther. She sat down. Tom rested with her, and they talked of home, and the friends there, and the comfortable beds and, above all, the light! Fatigue bore so heavily upon Becky that she drowsed off to sleep. Tom was grateful. He sat looking into her drawn face and saw it grow smooth and natural under the influence of pleasant dreams; and by and by a smile dawned and rested there. The peaceful face reflected somewhat of peace and healing into his own spirit, and his thoughts wandered away to dreamy memories. While he was deep in his musings, Becky woke up with a little laugh—but it was stricken dead upon her lips, and a groan followed.

"Oh, how *could* I sleep! I wish I never, never had waked! No! No, I don't, Tom! Don't look so! I won't say it again."

They rose up and wandered along, hand in hand and hopeless. A long time after this—they could not tell how long—Tom said they must go softly and listen for dripping water—they must find a spring. They found one presently, and sat down, and Tom fastened his candle to the wall in front of them with some clay.

Becky said, "Tom, I am so hungry."

Tom took something out of his pocket. "Do you remember this?"

Becky almost smiled. "It's our wedding cake, Tom."

"Yes—I wish it was as big as a barrel, for it's all we've got."

"I saved it from the picnic for us to dream on, Tom, the way grown-up people do with wedding cake—but it'll be our—"

She dropped the sentence where it was. Tom divided the cake and Becky ate with good appetite, while he nibbled at his moiety. There was abundance of cold water to finish the feast with. By and by Becky suggested that they move on again. Tom was silent a moment. Then he said:

"Becky, can you bear it if I tell you something?"

Becky's face paled, but she thought she could.

"Well, then, Becky, we must stay here, where there's water to drink. That little piece is our last candle!"

Becky gave loose to tears; but at length she said, "Tom, they'll miss us and hunt for us! Maybe they're hunting now."

"I reckon maybe they are. I hope they are."

"When would they miss us, Tom?"

"When they get back to the boat, I reckon."

"Tom, it might be dark—would they notice we hadn't come?"

"I don't know. But anyway, your mother would miss you as soon as they got home."

A frightened look in Becky's face made Tom see that he had made a blunder. Becky was not to have gone home that night! The Sabbath morning might be half spent before Mrs. Thatcher discovered that Becky was not at Mrs. Harper's.

The children fastened their eyes upon their bit of candle and watched it melt pitilessly away; saw the half inch of wick stand alone at last; saw the feeble flame rise and fall, climb the thin column of smoke, linger at its top a moment, and then—the horror of utter darkness reigned!

After what seemed a mighty stretch of time, both awoke out of a dead stupor of sleep and resumed their miseries once more. Tom said it might be Sunday, now—maybe Monday. He said that they must have been missed long ago, and no doubt the search was going on. He would shout and maybe someone would come. He tried it; but in the darkness the distant echoes sounded so hideous that he tried it no more.

The hours wasted away, and hunger came to torment the captives again. A portion of Tom's half of the cake was left; they divided and ate it. But they seemed hungrier than before.

By and by Tom said, "*Sh!* Did you hear that?"

Both held their breath and listened. There was a sound like the faintest, far-off shout. Instantly Tom answered it, and, leading Becky by the hand, started groping down the corridor in its direction. Presently he listened again; again the sound was heard, and apparently a little nearer. "It's them!" said Tom. "Come along, Becky—we're all right now!"

The joy of the prisoners was almost overwhelming. Their speed was slow, however, because pitfalls were common, and had to be guarded against. They shortly came to one and had to stop. It might be three feet deep, it might be a hundred—there was no passing it, at any rate. Tom got down on his breast and reached as far as he could. No bottom. They must stay there until the searchers came. They listened; evidently the distant shoutings were growing more distant! A moment or two more and they had gone altogether. Tom whooped until he was hoarse, but it was of no use.

The children groped their way back to the spring. They slept again, and awoke famished and woe-stricken. Tom believed it must be Tuesday by this time.

Now an idea struck him. There were some side passages near at hand. It would be better to explore some of these than bear the weight of the heavy time in idleness. He took a kite line from his pocket, tied it to a projection, and he and Becky started, Tom in the lead, unwinding the line as he groped along.

At the end of twenty steps the corridor ended in a "jumping-off place." Tom got down on his knees and felt below, and then as far around the corner as he could reach with his hands; he made an effort to stretch yet a little farther to the right, and at that moment, not twenty yards away, a human hand, holding a candle, appeared from behind a rock! Tom lifted up a glorious shout, and instantly that hand was followed by the body it belonged to—Injun Joe's! Tom was paralyzed. He was vastly gratified the next moment to see the "Spaniard" take to his heels out of sight. Tom wondered that Joe had not recognized his voice and come and killed him for testifying in court. But the echoes must have disguised the voice. He was careful to keep from Becky what it was he had seen. He told her he had only shouted "for luck."

But hunger and wretchedness rise superior to fears in the long run. Another tedious wait at the spring and another long sleep brought changes. The children awoke tortured with hunger. Tom proposed to explore another passage. He felt willing to risk Injun Joe and all other terrors. But Becky had sunk into a dreary apathy. She said she would wait, now, where she was, and die; but she implored him to come back every little while and speak to her, and she made him promise that when the awful time came, he would stay by her and hold her hand until it was over.

Tom kissed her, choking; then he took the kite line in his hand and went groping down one of the passages on his hands and knees, distressed with hunger and bodings of coming doom.

CHAPTER XVI

TUESDAY AFTERNOON CAME, and waned to the twilight. The village of St. Petersburg still mourned. Public prayers had been offered up for the lost children, but still no good news came from the cave. The majority of the searchers had gone back to their daily vocations, saying that it was plain the children could never be found. Mrs. Thatcher was ill. Aunt Polly had drooped into a settled melancholy, and her gray hair had grown almost white. The village went to its rest on Tuesday night sad and forlorn.

Away in the middle of the night a wild peal burst from the village bells, and in a moment the streets were swarming with half-clad people, who shouted, "Turn out! Turn out! They're found!" Tin pans and horns were added to the din, the population moved toward the river, met the children coming in an open carriage, thronged around it, joined its homeward march, and swept magnificently up the main street roaring huzzah after huzzah!

The village was illuminated; nobody went to bed again; it was the greatest night the little town had ever seen. A procession of villagers filed through Judge Thatcher's house, seized and kissed the saved ones, squeezed Mrs. Thatcher's hand, tried to speak but couldn't—and drifted out raining tears all over the place.

Aunt Polly's happiness was complete, and Mrs. Thatcher's nearly so. It would be complete, however, as soon as the messenger dispatched with the great news to the cave should get the word to her husband. Tom lay upon a sofa with an eager auditory about him and told the history of the adventure, putting in many striking additions to adorn it withal; and closed with a description of how he left Becky and went on an exploring expedition; how he followed two avenues as far as his kite line would reach; how he followed a third to the fullest stretch of the kite line, and was about to turn back when he glimpsed a far-off speck that looked like daylight; dropped the line and groped toward it, pushed his hand and shoulders through a small hole and saw the broad Mississippi rolling by! And how if it had only happened to be night he would not have seen that speck of daylight or explored that passage any more! He told how he went back for Becky and how they pushed their way out at the hole; how they sat there and cried for gladness; how some men came along in a skiff and Tom hailed them; how the men didn't believe the wild tale at first, "because," said they, "you are five miles down the river below the valley the cave is in"—then took them aboard, rowed to a house, gave them supper, made them rest, and then brought them home.

Before daydawn, Judge Thatcher and the handful of searchers with him were tracked out, in the cave, by the twine clues they had strung behind them, and informed of the great news.

Three days and nights of toil and hunger in the cave were not to be shaken off at once, as Tom and Becky soon discovered. They were bedridden all of Wednesday and Thursday, and seemed to grow more tired and worn all the time. Tom got about a little on Thursday, was downtown Friday, and nearly as whole as ever Saturday; but Becky did not leave her room until Sunday, and then she looked as if she had passed through a wasting illness.

Tom learned of Huck's sickness and went to see him on Friday, but could not be admitted to the bedroom; neither could he on Saturday. He was admitted after that, but was warned to keep still about his adventure and introduce no exciting topic. The Widow Douglas stayed by to see that he obeyed. At home Tom learned of the Cardiff Hill event; also that the "ragged man's" body had been found in the river near the ferry landing; he had been drowned while trying to escape, perhaps.

About a fortnight after Tom's rescue from the cave, he stopped at Judge Thatcher's house to see Becky. The Judge had some friends there, and someone asked Tom ironically if he wouldn't like to go to the cave again. Tom said he thought he wouldn't mind. The Judge said, "Well, there are others like you, Tom. But we have taken care of that. Nobody will get lost in that cave anymore."

"Why?"

"Because I had its big door sheathed with boiler iron two weeks ago, and triple-locked—and I've got the keys."

Tom turned as white as a sheet.

"What's the matter, boy! Here, somebody! Fetch water!"

The water was brought and thrown into Tom's face.

"Ah, now you're all right. What was the matter with you, Tom?"

"Oh, Judge, Injun Joe's in the cave!"

WITHIN A FEW MINUTES the news had spread, and a dozen skiff-loads of men were on their way to McDougal's Cave. Tom Sawyer was in the skiff that bore Judge Thatcher.

When the cave door was unlocked, a sorrowful sight presented itself. Injun Joe lay stretched upon the ground, dead, with his face close to the crack of the door, as if his longing eyes had been fixed, to the latest moment, upon the light of the free world outside. Tom was touched, for he knew by his own experience how this wretch had suffered; but nevertheless he felt an abounding sense of relief and security, now, which revealed to him how vast a weight of dread had been lying upon him since the day he lifted his voice against this bloody-minded outcast.

Injun Joe was buried near the mouth of the cave, and people flocked there from all the towns and farms for miles around; and they confessed that they had almost as satisfactory a time at the funeral as they could have had at the hanging.

The morning after the funeral Tom took Huck to a private place. Huck had grown plenty strong enough, now, to hear exciting talk. He had learned all about Tom's adventure from the Welshman and the Widow Douglas, by this time, but Tom said he reckoned there was one thing they had not told him. Huck's face saddened. He said:

"I know what it is. You got into Number Two and never found anything but whiskey. I just knowed it must 'a' ben you; and I knowed you hadn't got the money, becuz if you had, you'd 'a' got at me someway or other and told me. Tom, something's always told me we'd never get holt of that swag."

"Why, Huck, *I* never told on that tavern keeper. *You* know his tavern was all right the Saturday I went to the picnic. Don't you remember you was to watch there that night?"

"Oh, yes! It was that very night that I follered Injun Joe to the widder's."

"*You* followed him?"

"Yes—but you keep mum. I reckon Injun Joe's left friends behind him, and I don't want 'em doing me mean tricks."

Then Huck told his entire adventure in confidence to Tom, who had only heard of the Welshmen's part of it before.

"Well," said Huck, presently, "whoever nipped the whiskey in Number Two nipped the money, too, I reckon."

"Huck, that money wasn't ever in Number Two!"

"What!" Huck searched his comrade's face. "Tom, have you got on the track of that money again?"

"Huck, it's in the cave!"

Huck's eyes blazed. "Tom—honest injun, now—is it fun or earnest?"

"Earnest, Huck—will you go in there with me and help get it?"

"I will if it's where we can blaze our way to it and not get lost!"

"Huck, we can do that without the least little trouble. Are you strong enough to go right now?"

"Is it far in the cave, Tom? I ben on my pins a little, three days, now, but I don't think I could walk more'n a mile."

"It's about five mile into there the way anybody but me would go, Huck, but there's a mighty short cut that they don't anybody but me know about. Huck, I'll take you right to it in a skiff."

"Let's start right off, Tom."

"All right. We want some bread and meat, and a bag or two, and two or three kite strings, and some of these newfangled things they call lucifer matches. I tell you, many's the time I wished I had some when I was in there before."

A trifle after noon the boys borrowed a small skiff from a citizen who was absent, and got under way. When they were several miles below Cave Hollow, Tom said, "Now you see this bluff here looks all alike all the way down from the hollow—no houses, bushes all alike. But do you see that white place up yonder where there's been a landslide? Well, that's one of my marks. We'll get ashore, now."

They landed.

"Now, Huck, where we're a-standing you could touch that hole I got out of with a fishing pole. See if you can find it."

Huck searched and found nothing. Tom proudly marched into a clump of sumac and said, "Here you are! Look at it, Huck; it's the snuggest hole in this country. You just keep mum about it. All along I've been wanting to be a robber, but I knew I'd got to have a thing like this, and where to run across it was the bother. We've got it now, and we'll keep it quiet, only we'll let Joe Harper and Ben Rogers in—because of course there's got to be a gang, or there wouldn't be any style about it. Tom Sawyer's Gang—it sounds splendid, don't it, Huck?"

"Well, it just does, Tom. It's real bully. I bleeve it's better'n to be a pirate."

"Yes, it's better in some ways, because it's close to home and circuses and all that."

By this time everything was ready and the boys entered the hole, Tom in the lead. They toiled to the farther end of the tunnel, then made their spliced kite strings fast and moved on. A few steps brought them to the spring, and Tom felt a shudder quiver all through him. He showed Huck the fragment of candlewick perched on a lump of clay against the wall, and described how he and Becky had watched the flame struggle and expire.

The boys began to quiet down to whispers, now, for the stillness and gloom of the place oppressed their spirits. They went on, and presently followed Tom's other corridor until they reached the "jumping-off place." The candles revealed the fact that it was not really a precipice, but only a steep clay hill twenty feet high. Tom whispered, "Now I'll show you something." He held his candle aloft. "Look as far around the corner as you can. There, see—on the big rock over yonder—done with candle smoke."

"Tom, it's a *cross!*"

"*Now* where's your Number Two? *Under the cross*, hey? Right yonder's where I saw Injun Joe poke up his candle, Huck!"

Huck stared at the mystic sign awhile, and then said with a shaky voice, "Tom, let's git out of here!"

"What! And leave the treasure?"

"Yes—leave it. Injun Joe's ghost is round about there, certain."

"No it ain't, Huck. It would ha'nt the place where he died."

"No, Tom, it wouldn't. It would hang round the money."

Misgivings gathered in Tom's mind. But presently an idea occurred to him—"Looky here, Huck, Injun Joe's ghost ain't a-going to come around where there's a cross!"

The point was well taken. It had its effect.

"Tom, I didn't think of that. But that's so. I reckon we'll climb down there and have a hunt for that box."

Tom went first, cutting rude steps in the clay hill as he descended. Huck followed. Four avenues opened out of the small cavern where the great rock stood. The boys examined three of them with no result. They found a small recess in the one nearest the base of the rock, with a pallet of blankets in it; also an old suspender and the well-gnawed bones of two or three fowl. But there was no money box. Tom said, "He said *under* the cross. Well, this comes nearest to being under the cross. It can't be under the rock itself, because that sets solid on the ground."

They searched everywhere once more, and then sat down, discouraged. By and by Tom said, "Looky here, Huck, there's footprints and some candle grease on the clay about one side of this rock, but not on the other sides. Now, what's that for? I bet you the money *is* under the rock. I'm going to dig in the clay."

"That ain't no bad notion, Tom!" said Huck.

Tom's "real Barlow" was out at once, and he had not dug four inches before he struck wood. "Hey, Huck! You hear that?"

Huck began to dig and scratch now. Some boards were soon uncovered and removed. They had concealed a natural chasm which led under the rock. Tom got into this and held out his candle, but he could not see to the end of the rift. He stooped and passed under with Huck at his heels; the narrow way descended gradually. Then Tom turned a short curve and exclaimed, "My goodness, Huck, looky here!"

It was the treasure box, sure enough, occupying a snug little cavern, along with an empty powder keg, a couple of guns in leather cases, two or three pairs of old moccasins, a belt, and some other rubbish well soaked with the water drip.

"Got it at last!" said Huck, plowing among the tarnished coins with his hand. "My, but we're rich, Tom!"

"Huck, I always reckoned we'd get it. It's just too good to believe, but we *have* got it, sure! Say—let's not fool around here. Let's snake it out. Lemme see if I can lift the box."

It weighed about fifty pounds. Tom could lift it, but could not carry it. "I thought so," he said. "*They* carried it like it was heavy, that day at the ha'nted house. I reckon I was right to fetch the bags along."

The money was soon in the bags and the boys took it up to the cross rock.

"Now let's fetch the guns and things," said Huck.

"No, Huck—leave them there. They're just the tricks to have when we go to robbing. We'll keep them there, and we'll hold our orgies there, too. It's an awful snug place for orgies."

"What orgies?"

"*I* dono. But robbers always have orgies. Come along, Huck; it's getting late. I'm hungry. We'll eat in the skiff."

They presently emerged into the clump of sumac, looked warily out, found the coast clear, and were soon lunching in the skiff. As the sun dipped toward the horizon they got under way. Tom skimmed up the shore through the long twilight, chatting cheerily with Huck, and landed shortly after dark.

"Now, Huck," said Tom, "we'll hide the money in the loft of the widow's woodshed, and I'll come up in the morning and we'll count it and divide, and then we'll hunt up a place out in the woods for it where it will be safe. Just you lay quiet here and watch the stuff till I run and hook Benny Taylor's little wagon; I won't be gone a minute."

He presently returned with the wagon, put the sacks into it, threw some old rags on top of them and started off, dragging his cargo behind him. When the boys reached the Welshman's house, the Welshman stepped out and said, "Hello, who's that?"

"Huck and Tom Sawyer."

"Good! Come along with me, boys; you are keeping everybody waiting. Here—hurry up, trot ahead—I'll haul the wagon. Why, it's not as light as it might be. Got bricks in it? Or old metal?"

"Old metal," said Tom.

"I judged so. The boys in this town will fool away more time hunting up six bits' worth of old iron to sell to the foundry than they would to make twice the money at regular work. But that's human nature—hurry along, hurry along!"

Huck wanted to know what the hurry was about.

"Never mind; you'll see when we get to the Widow Douglas's."

A little later Huck found himself pushed, along with Tom, into Mrs. Douglas's drawing room. Mr. Jones, the Welshman, left the wagon near the door and followed.

The place was grandly lighted, and everybody that was of any consequence in the village was there. The Thatchers were there, the Harpers, the Rogerses, Aunt Polly, Sid, Mary, the minister, and a great many more, and all dressed in their best. The widow received the boys as heartily as anyone could well receive two such looking beings. They were covered with clay and candle grease. Aunt Polly blushed crimson with humiliation, and frowned at Tom. Nobody suffered half as much as the two boys did, however. Mr. Jones said, "Tom wasn't at home yet, so I gave him up; but I stumbled on him and Huck right at my door, and so I just brought them along."

"You did just right," said the widow. "Come with me, boys."

She took them to a bedchamber and said, "Now wash and dress yourselves. Here are two new suits of clothes—shirts, socks, everything. They're Huck's—no, no thanks, Huck—Mr. Jones bought one and I the other. But they'll fit both of you. Get into them. We'll wait—come down when you are slicked up enough."

Then she left, and Huck said, "Tom, we can slope, if we can find a rope. The window ain't high from the ground."

"Shucks, what do you want to slope for?"

"Well, I ain't used to that kind of a crowd. I ain't going down there, Tom."

"Oh, bother! It ain't anything. I'll take care of you."

Sid appeared. "Tom," said he, "Auntie has been waiting for you all afternoon. Say—ain't this grease and clay on your clothes?"

"Now, Mr. Siddy, you jist 'tend to your own business. What's all this blowout about, anyway?"

"It's one of the widow's parties that she's always having. This time it's for the Welshman and his sons, on account of that scrape they helped her out of. And say—I can tell you something, if you want to know."

"Well, what?"

"Why, old Mr. Jones is going to try to spring something on the people here tonight, but I overheard him tell Auntie today about it, as a secret, but I reckon it's not much of a secret *now*. Everybody knows—the widow, too, for all she tries to let on she don't. Mr. Jones was bound Huck should be here—couldn't get along with his grand secret without Huck, you know!"

"Secret about what, Sid?"

"About Huck tracking the robbers to the widow's. I reckon Mr. Jones was going to make a grand time over his surprise, but I bet you it will drop pretty flat." Sid chuckled in a contented way.

"Sid, was it you that told?"

"Oh, never mind who it was. *Somebody* told—that's enough."

"Sid, there's only one person in this town mean enough to do that, and that's you. You can't do any but mean things, and you can't bear to see anybody praised for doing good ones. There—no thanks, as the widow says"—and Tom cuffed Sid's ears and helped him to the door with several kicks. "Now go and tell Auntie if you dare!"

Some minutes later the widow's guests were at the supper table, and a dozen children were propped up at little side tables in the same room, after the fashion of that country and that day. At the proper time Mr. Jones made his little speech, in which he thanked the widow for the honor she was doing himself and his sons, but said that there was another person whose modesty—

And so forth and so on. He sprung his secret about Huck's share in the adventure in a fine dramatic manner, but the surprise it occasioned was largely counterfeit. However, the widow made a pretty fair show of astonishment, and heaped so many compliments upon Huck that he almost forgot the nearly intolerable discomfort of his new clothes in the entirely intolerable discomfort of being set up as a target for everybody's gaze and laudations.

The widow said she meant to give Huck a home under her roof and have him educated; and that when she could spare the money she would start him in business. Tom's chance was come. He said, "Huck don't need it. Huck's rich."

Nothing but a heavy strain upon the good manners of the company kept back the proper complimentary laugh at this pleasant joke. But the silence was a little awkward. Tom broke it. "Oh, you needn't smile—I reckon I can show you. You just wait a minute."

Tom ran out of doors. The company looked at each other—and looked inquiringly at Huck, who was tongue-tied.

"Sid, what ails Tom?" said Aunt Polly. "I never—"

Tom entered, struggling with the weight of his sacks, and Aunt Polly did not finish her sentence. Tom poured the mass of yellow coin upon the table and said, "There—what did I tell you? Half of it's Huck's and half of it's mine!"

All gazed, nobody spoke for a moment. Then there was a unanimous call for an explanation. Tom said he could furnish it, and he did. The tale was long, but brimful of interest. There was no interruption to break the charm of its flow.

When he had finished, Mr. Jones said, "I thought I had fixed up a little surprise for this occasion, but it don't amount to anything now. This one makes it sing mighty small, I'll allow."

The money was counted. The sum amounted to over twelve thousand dollars.

CHAPTER XVII

THE READER MAY REST satisfied that Tom's and Huck's windfall made a mighty stir in the poor little village of St. Petersburg. So vast a sum, in actual cash, seemed next to incredible. It was talked about, gloated over, glorified, until the reason of many of the citizens tottered under the strain of the unhealthy excitement. Every "haunted" house in St. Petersburg and the neighboring villages was dissected, plank by plank, and ransacked for hidden treasure—and not by boys, but men—pretty grave, unromantic men, too, some of them. Wherever Tom and Huck appeared they were courted, admired, stared at. All their sayings were treasured and repeated; everything they did seemed to be regarded as remarkable; moreover, their past history was raked up and discovered to bear marks of conspicuous originality.

The Widow Douglas put Huck's money out at six percent, and Judge Thatcher did the same with Tom's at Aunt Polly's request. Each lad had an income, now, that was simply prodigious—a dollar for every weekday in the year and half of the Sundays. It was just what the minister got—no, it was what he was promised—he generally couldn't collect it. A dollar and a quarter a week would board, lodge and school a boy in those old simple days—and clothe him and wash him, too, for that matter.

Judge Thatcher had conceived a great opinion of Tom. He said that no commonplace boy would ever have got his daughter out of the cave. The Judge hoped to see Tom a great lawyer or a great soldier someday, and he said he meant to look to it that Tom should be admitted to the national military academy and afterward trained in the best law school in the country, in order that he might be ready for either career or both. When Becky told her father, in strict confidence, how Tom had taken her whipping at school, the Judge was visibly moved; and when she pleaded grace for the mighty lie which Tom had told in order to shift that whipping from her shoulders to his own, the Judge said with a fine outburst that it was a noble, a generous, a magnanimous lie.

Huck Finn's wealth and the fact that he was now under the Widow Douglas's protection introduced him into society—no, dragged him into it, hurled him into it—and his sufferings were almost more than he could bear. The widow's servants kept him clean and neat, combed and brushed. He had to eat with knife and fork; he had to go to church; he had to talk so properly that speech was become insipid in his mouth.

He bravely bore his miseries three weeks, and then one day turned up missing. For forty-eight hours the widow hunted for him everywhere in great distress. The public were profoundly concerned; they searched high and low. Early the third morning Tom Sawyer wisely went poking among some old empty hogsheads down behind the abandoned slaughterhouse, and in one of them he found the refugee. Huck had slept there; he had just breakfasted upon some stolen odds and ends of food, and was lying off, now, in comfort, with his pipe. He was unkempt, uncombed, and clad in his old ruin of rags. Tom routed him out, told him the trouble he had been causing, and urged him to go home. Huck's face took a melancholy cast. He said:

"Don't talk about it, Tom. I've tried it, and it don't work. It ain't for me. The widder's good to me, and friendly, but I can't stand them ways. She makes me git up at the same time every morning; she makes me wash, and wear them blamed clothes that just smothers me. I got to go to church and—I hate them ornery sermons! I can't ketch a fly in there, I can't chaw, and I got to wear shoes all Sunday."

"Well, everybody does that way, Huck."

"Tom, it don't make no difference. I ain't everybody, and I can't *stand* it. It's awful to be tied up so. And grub comes too easy—I don't take no interest in vittles, that way. I got to ask to go a-fishing; I got to ask to go in a-swimming—dern'd if I hain't got to ask to do everything! I *had* to shove, Tom. And besides, that school's going to open, and I'd 'a' had to go to it—well, I wouldn't stand *that!* Looky here, Tom, being rich ain't what it's cracked up to be. It's just worry and worry, and sweat and sweat, and a-wishing you was dead all the time. Now these clothes suits me, and this bar'l suits me, and I ain't ever going to shake 'em anymore. Tom, I wouldn't ever got into all this trouble if it hadn't 'a' been for that money. Now you just take my sheer of it along with your'n, and gimme a ten-center sometimes—not many times, becuz I don't give a dern for a thing 'thout it's tollable hard to git—and you go and beg off for me with the widder."

"Oh, Huck, you know I can't do that. 'Tain't fair; and besides, if you'll try this thing just a while longer you'll come to like it."

"Like it! Yes—the way I'd like a hot stove if I was to set on it long enough. No, Tom, I won't be rich, and I won't live in them cussed smothery houses. I like the woods, and the river, and hogs-heads. Blame it all! Just as we'd got guns, and a cave, and all just fixed to rob, here this dern foolishness has got to come up and spile it all!"

Tom saw his opportunity— "Looky here, Huck, being rich ain't going to keep me back from turning robber."

"No! Oh, good licks, are you in deadwood earnest, Tom?"

"Just as dead earnest as I'm a-sitting here. But, Huck, we can't let you into the gang if you ain't respectable, you know."

Huck's joy was quenched. "Can't let me in, Tom? Didn't you let me go for a pirate?"

"Yes, but that's different. A robber is more high-toned than a pirate—as a general thing."

"Now, Tom, hain't you always ben friendly to me? You wouldn't shet me out, would you, Tom?"

"Huck, I wouldn't want to, and I *don't* want to—but what would people say? Why, they'd say, 'Mph! Tom Sawyer's Gang! Pretty low characters in it!' They'd mean you, Huck."

Huck was silent, engaged in a mental struggle. Finally he said, "Well, I'll go back to the widder for a month and see if I can come to stand it, if you'll let me b'long to the gang, Tom."

"All right, Huck, it's a whiz! Come along, and I'll ask the widow to let up on you a little."

"Will you, Tom? That's good. If she'll let up on some of the roughest things, I'll cuss private, and crowd through or bust. When you going to start the gang?"

"Oh, right off. We'll get the boys together and have the initia-tion tonight, maybe."

"What's that?"

"It's to swear to stand by one another, and never tell the gang's secrets, even if you're chopped all to flinders, and kill anybody and all his family that hurts one of the gang."

"That's gay—that's mighty gay, Tom, I tell you."

"Well, I bet it is. And all that swearing's got to be done at midnight, in the lonesomest, awfulest place you can find—a ha'nted house is the best, but they're all ripped up now."

"Well, midnight's good, anyway, Tom."

"Yes, so it is. And you've got to swear on a coffin, and sign it with blood."

"Now, that's something *like!* Why, it's a million times bullier than pirating. I'll stick to the widder till I rot, Tom; and if I git to be a reg'lar ripper of a robber, and everybody talking about it, I reckon she'll be proud she snaked me in out of the wet."

CONCLUSION

So ENDETH THIS CHRONICLE. It being strictly a history of a *boy*, it must stop here; the story could not go much further without becoming the history of a *man*. When one writes a novel about grown people, he knows exactly where to stop—that is, with a marriage; but when he writes of juveniles, he must stop where he best can.

Other Titles by Mark Twain

A Connecticut Yankee in King Arthur's Court. New York: Bantam, 1983.

Great Short Works of Mark Twain. New York: Harper & Row, 1967.

The Innocents Abroad. New York: New American Library, 1980.

Letters from the Earth. New York: Harper & Row, 1962.

Life on the Mississippi. New York: Penguin, 1985.

The Mysterious Stranger & Other Stories. New York: New American Library, 1962.

A Pen Warmed Up in Hell. New York: Harper & Row, 1979.

The Prince and the Pauper. New York: Bantam, 1983.

Pudd'nhead Wilson. New York: Penguin, 1969.

Tom Sawyer Abroad & Tom Sawyer, Detective. Berkeley: University of California Press, 1981.

The Unabridged Mark Twain. Philadelphia: Running Press, 1975.

The Unabridged Mark Twain, No. 2. Lawrence Teacher, editor. Philadelphia: Running Press, 1979.